Jack of Diamonds

Other Books By Meredith Bond

<u>The Merry Men Series</u>
An Exotic Heir
A Merry Marquis
A Rake's Reward
A Dandy in Disguise
My Lord Ghost
My Gentleman Thief
Under the Mango Tree
A Spanish Dilemma
When Hearts Rebel

<u>The Storm Series</u>
Storm on the Horizon
Bridging the Storm
Magic in the Storm
Through the Storm

<u>The Children of Avalon Trilogy</u>
Air: Merlin's Chalice
Water: The Return of Excalibur
Fire: Nimuë's Destiny

<u>The Ladies' Wagering Whist Society</u>
A Hand for the Duke
Jack of Diamonds
The Games She Played

Falling
Falling for a Pirate

Chapter One: A Fast, Fun Way to Write Fiction
Self-Publishing: Easy as ABC
"In A Beginning", a short story featuring Lilith

Jack of Diamonds

The Ladies' Wagering Whist Society

Book Two

Meredith Bond

Cover Art by QuarterbackTB, https://qtbdesign.wixsite.com/qtbdesign

Logo by Anjali Banerji

Edited by The Editing Hall, http://theeditinghall.com

Published by Anessa Books, http://anessabooks.com

Chapter One

~May 10, 1806~

Lydia Sheffield grasped onto her friend Tina's arm, certain that she had to be imagining things. "I'm sorry, but did you just see that?"

"See what?" Tina asked, following her line of sight.

"That man." Lydia followed the man with her eyes across the crowded ballroom, trying to indicate who she was speaking about without outright pointing in his direction. "That man heading out the door, the one in the gray coat. He just stole two diamond pins from a lady's hair!"

"What? You must be imagining things, Miss Sheffield," said Lady Norman, Tina's mother, with a little laugh. "No gentleman would steal pins from a lady's hair!"

"No, I'm certain... Oh, he's gone," Lydia said, feeling strangely disappointed. She let go of Tina's arm, but her heart was still pounding. She'd never actually witnessed a crime before.

"He must have just accidentally bumped into her," Tina said.

"Yes," Lydia said, not believing it for a second. "Perhaps it was that." Truly, who would steal hairpins from a lady at a ball? No one could possibly be so brazen! Besides which, everyone here had been invited, and no member of the ton would be so desperate that they would resort to stealing. No, Tina was right. She had to have imagined it.

Lydia turned back to Tina and her mother. "Yes, you must be right." She forced out a little laugh. "No one would steal hairpins from a lady at a ball." She shook her head, trying to dispel the image from her mind's eye.

"Perhaps you need some fresh air as much as I do," Tina suggested.

"Oh, no. I'm fine. Truly," Lydia said, giving another laugh. What she really wanted to do was follow the man and see where he went. But there was no way to do so politely. No, she was stuck right where she was.

"Well, then, if you don't mind, I think I'm going to get step outside for a moment. If one more person insults me to my face, I'm not entirely certain I won't actually scream," Tina said, putting on a brave smile.

"Oh, dear!" her mother said, looking a little worried.

"It's all right. I'm sure that a brief walk in the garden will make me feel better. If you'll excuse me." Tina gave them both a little curtsy and headed out the French doors to the garden.

Lydia had been doing her best to be a good friend to Tina Ayres when she'd imagined she'd seen the theft. Tina had just made her society debut that very evening and was having a hard time of it.

Lydia had been half-listening to Tina and her mother discuss how rude people could be when the man caught her eye. She'd been casually scanning the people crowding Lady Kershaw's ballroom when she noticed the gentleman move in what almost looked like a furtive manner behind a group of ladies.

The women were probably discussing poor Tina, as every once in a while one of them stole a glance in her direction. It was what nearly everyone at the party was talking about after all. Before today, Tina had been known to a number of ladies of the ton merely as a modiste—granted, she was one who made beautiful, extremely flattering gowns, but this evening her father, the Earl of Ayres, had re-introduced her as his daughter. But for Lydia, it was the gentleman in the gray coat who'd held her attention.

He was incredibly handsome in a rather ordinary way. He was of average height with dark blond hair. His clothing was completely ordinary, nothing spectacular, or particularly memorable. It was true that his face was handsome and his physique on the athletic side, but other than that he was completely forgettable. Lydia had just been trying to figure out what it was about him that captured her attention, when she'd seen him pluck the pin from one of the older ladies.

Lydia studied the woman's complicated coiffure. It was a maze of braids and curls all held together by a dozen or so diamond hairpins. *Had* the man—could she call him a gentleman?—pulled a pin from the lady's hair?

"I can't help but wonder who that gentleman was, though," Lydia said to Lady Norman after Tina left.

"Maybe I know him. What did he look like?" her friend asked, even though she was still watching her daughter's retreating back. Lady Norman was always so helpful and more than willing to step in as a sort of chaperone to Lydia since her father usually made himself scarce the moment they walked into any party.

Lydia pictured the gentleman in her mind. "He was tall but not very tall. Brown, maybe dark blond hair. He wore a dark gray coat and black waistcoat with gray embroidery. Quite elegant, actually, in a very understated way."

Lady Norman turned back to Lydia. "I don't believe I've seen the gentleman."

"Oh, well. It's all right. I'm sure I'll see him again."

"One always does," Lady Norman agreed.

It was less than a quarter of an hour later when Lydia did spy the gentleman again, and oddly enough, he was once again lurking among the ladies. How was it that they didn't notice him, Lydia wondered.

This time she was on her own, so she wound her way through the crowded ballroom, doing her best to keep an eye on the man. It wasn't easy and she did, in fact, lose sight of him when she was waylaid by Mrs. Aldridge. The lady was a member of the Ladies' Wagering Whist Society along with Lady Norman and herself.

Mrs. Aldridge looked quite fetching in a gown of deep pink with matching rubies circling her throat, wrists, and hanging from her ears. Lydia, never one to pass up such an opportunity, complimented her on her attire.

"Thank you, but why are you not dancing, Miss Sheffield?" Mrs. Aldridge asked in a good-natured scold.

Lydia gave the woman a wink. "I'm just on my way around the ballroom in the hopes of enticing a particular gentleman to ask me," she said with a giggle before continuing on her way.

The older woman burst out laughing but quickly stifled herself when heads turned her way.

Sadly, when Lydia turned back to where her quarry had been, the man had disappeared once again.

Lydia harrumphed to herself. This was definitely the most elusive gentleman she'd ever seen. She was just about to turn back toward Mrs. Aldridge when there was a small commotion among the ladies by whom he'd been loitering.

"I was certain I had it on when I went into the lady's retiring room," said one rather rotund woman in a dove gray silk dress.

"Perhaps it fell off when you washed your hands?" one of her companions asked.

"But I didn't…er, yes, perhaps that is the case. I'll just go back and see if anyone has found it," she said, turning slightly pink.

Lydia stepped up to the lady's friend and asked, "Is everything all right, my lady?"

"Oh yes, Lady Fostler has just misplaced her bracelet." The woman raised a lorgnette to her eyes and peered at Lydia. "Have we met?"

"Yes, the Duchess of Kendall introduced us at Lady Bradmore's ball a few weeks ago," she said, lying straight through her teeth but knowing no woman would ever deny knowledge of an introduction by a duchess. "I'm Lydia Sheffield. My father is Lord Daniel Sheffield,"

As expected the woman nodded slowly as she lowered her eyepiece. "Oh, yes, of course, Miss Sheffield. How lovely to see you again this evening."

"And you, my lady. I do hope that Lady Fostler finds her bracelet," Lydia said.

"As do I. It was apparently given to her by her husband for her birthday only last year. A beautiful diamond confection," the lady said.

"Oh, dear," Lydia tsked sadly. That gentleman in the gray coat… He wouldn't have… he couldn't have… Lydia shook her head. No! It would simply be too outrageous if he had stolen a bracelet right off a woman's wrist.

But Lydia was more determined than ever to discover the identity of the man.

~*~

John, the Viscount Welles, didn't like hiding behind potted plants. It made him feel ridiculous, and yet he had to make sure the girl who had been heading directly toward him a moment ago didn't see him. It wasn't that he didn't want to speak with her—goodness knows he'd love to—but not this evening. Not while he was working.

The girl was not only beautiful, but if he wasn't mistaken, she was the famous Miss Lydia Sheffield, considered one of the "diamonds" of the season. She was funny and charismatic—or so he'd heard. He'd never been introduced, and he knew he didn't want to be. She was precisely the sort of girl he avoided at all costs.

He wasn't quite sure how he'd drawn the attention of the lovely Miss Sheffield. He was dressed as always in his most unmemorable clothes. Black and gray, he'd found, usually encouraged eyes to slip right by him. His waistcoat was as understated as the rest of him, and carefully cultivated to be so.

Only a few years ago when he'd been at university, he'd dressed better. He'd been more outgoing and enjoyed his excursions to London as much as anyone in his group of friends, despite being "the quiet one". Then, the world was his to discover and enjoy.

So much had changed since those carefree days.

He no longer enjoyed being social, or so he told himself. He didn't have the time or inclination to stand about and discuss silly things like who danced with whom or who was seen riding in the park with another. No, now he simply hid behind plants, avoiding beautiful women instead of seeking them out. Now, he was stealing jewels straight out of the hair of ladies and off their wrists without them even realizing what had happened.

In a way, he hated taking advantage of unsuspecting people, but on the other hand, he rather enjoyed the challenge of relieving the wealthy of their jewels. After years of practice, he could lift a piece from its owner without them ever realizing it. There was a thrill to it, of course, but more importantly, it allowed him to do so much more for the poor than so many of his peers.

But in order to continue with his chosen occupation, he had to avoid the likes of Miss Lydia Sheffield, no matter how much he'd much rather be laughing and dancing with her.

Chapter Two

~May 11~

The next night, Mr. Meir was waiting in the far corner of the taproom of the Angel when John came in. No matter how early John came, Mr. Meir was always at the same table. John wondered if the fellow didn't stay at the tavern while he was in London. He didn't think there were rooms for rent, but perhaps he was mistaken.

"Good evening," the man said as John approached the slender gentleman dressed all in brown.

"A good evening to you, sir." They almost never used names, nor did Mr. Meir even call John "my lord." It was safer that way. No one listening to their conversation would be able to say who they were.

"Have you had a good week?" Mr. Meir asked, raising a finger to call the barmaid over. His wire-rimmed spectacles magnified the size of the gentleman's eyes giving them an odd, distorted sort of look.

"I have, thank you." John waited while two ales were ordered and then delivered.

He took a long draft of his once it was set in front of him. When he put his mug back down on the table, he made sure the paper packet he'd slipped onto the table was well hidden behind both the large tankard and his arm.

When his companion put his own mug down, the packet had shifted to behind it, and within moments it had disappeared altogether into a pocket of the man's greatcoat. Hardly a minute had passed between the time John had removed it from his own coat and the time it had disappeared again.

"My friend greatly appreciates the quality you are able to procure for him," Mr. Meir said.

"I'm glad to hear that. And also happy that he does such fine work as well," John commented. Mr. Meir's "friend" was a jeweler in Amsterdam who took the pieces John provided him, broke them apart, resold the diamonds, and melted down the gold for reuse. No one would ever be able to trace the stones back to their source, and no one in London would ever know what happened to the pieces that disappeared from time to time among the ton. It was a foolproof operation, and John felt lucky to have fallen into it.

An envelope appeared on the table in front of John. He quickly and unobtrusively slipped it into his pocket.

"For the packet you delivered last time," Mr. Meir said with a pleasant smile. He looked like a man John could potentially become friends with.

He had an agreeable disposition and shared an interest in the fascinating history of the Holy Roman Empire. Once their business had concluded, they'd spent a number of very pleasant evenings discussing the various emperors and the benefits, or lack thereof, of additions to the empire over the years.

The man's sunken cheeks filled out pleasantly when he smiled, and his dull gray eyes positively twinkled when he became passionate about whatever point he happened to be arguing. But before they could move on to more pleasant topics, it seemed as if he had something more he needed to convey to John.

The man fiddled with his tankard of ale. "My contact has written to me and wishes me to return as soon as possible. He's eager for what you've brought," Mr. Meir said before lifting the mug to his lips.

John nodded.

"But I need more to make my trip even more worthwhile. You understand, I'm sure," he said, wiping his mouth with the back of his hand.

John drew his eyebrows down over his eyes. "I'm not certain... How much more?"

"At least three, perhaps four more pieces. Can you do that?"

John sat back and thought about what events were coming up on the social schedule. There weren't many to which he was invited—one of the drawbacks of being an unassuming person. At least he still had friends from his university days who still remembered him fondly and the way he used to be. Perhaps now, however, he should use a different tactic. Perhaps something a little more direct than merely taking what was on offer at society parties.

"I'll see what I can do, but you understand that I can't make any assurances," John said.

"Naturally," his companion nodded.

John drained the last of his ale. "Very well, then. I'll send word if I am successful."

Mr. Meir nodded and then gave John a little smile. "On to more pleasant subjects?"

John gave a little laugh and a nod.

Mr. Meir proceeded to regale him with all that he'd read in a book he'd recently purchased, a new work focusing on the reach of the Holy Roman Empire into the more northern countries of Europe.

After an hour or so of very pleasant conversation and debate, John finished off his second tankard of ale and said goodnight to his companion. He still had some work to do that evening before returning home.

He stopped for a word with the proprietor of the tavern, leaving some coins with him should there be any sort of emergency that needed to be handled when he wasn't around. They'd gotten to know each other well over the past few years, and John trusted him enough to look after the interests of the people in the neighborhood. They were Mr. Miller's clientele. If they suffered, so did he.

John's stroll through the Rookeries afterward churned his stomach and not just because of the stench of gin and humanity. It was the women and babes huddled in doorways, the street urchins who attempted to pick his pockets of anything of value, and the men staggering down the alleyways having just drunk their day's wages, their hungry families be damned.

There were too many. He couldn't possibly help them all. John knew that, so he did what he could with the money he got from his thievery. He didn't keep a penny of the money he earned from Mr. Meir, but gave it all to those who needed it the most.

A discreet knock on a door next to a grocer's brought the man to the door. He wore neither a coat nor waistcoat. His shirt was untucked and open at the neck.

"Good evening to you, Mr. Cartwright," John said with a smile.

"Ah! Good evening, good evening, sir!" The man lost the suspicious look on his face immediately upon seeing who it was banging on his door so late at night.

"Would you have any outstanding debts owed to you this evening?" John asked as he always did.

"I do. Just one moment and I'll get my books. Come in," he said, stepping back and inviting John into the hall. Stairs led straight up to the grocer's apartments above the shop. John followed the gentleman up and into a cheerful, if dingy, little drawing room. A boy of about four sat playing on the bare wooden floor with a small wooden horse. Two stones stood in for more horses, and John made a mental note to himself to pick up a few more toys for the lad the next time he was on Bond Street.

The boy's mother sat stitching, leaning dangerously close to a candle, the only source of light in the room.

"Good evening, Mistress Cartwright," John said, giving her a small bow.

"Oh, good evening, sir, how lovely it is to see you," she said, smiling up at him. "You will forgive me for not getting up?"

"Of course. You go on with your work. I will be gone in but a moment after I have done some business with your husband." He turned toward the child and knelt down next to him. "And I brought a little something for you if your mother doesn't mind." He pulled a napkin from one of his pockets and handed it to the child.

"Thank you, sir!" the child said, opening it. A pile of fruit tarts spilled out, but John caught them before they hit the floor.

"I think there might be enough there for you to share with your parents if you are of a mind," John said with a wink.

"Oh, you are too good to us, sir, too good!" his mother said with a chuckle.

"It's my pleasure." John stood up and turned toward the grocer who had come in with his account books.

"Here you are, sir. Mrs. Brown, Mary Small, and little Johnny No Ear each owe us for groceries for the past two weeks totaling twelve shillings, four pence." The man showed him the accounts.

John looked them over briefly and then handed over a pound. "That should take care of that, and keep the extra so Mrs. Cartwright can have another candle or two."

"Oh, you are so good to us, sir. Thank you," the lady said with a giggle.

"Indeed. It's much appreciated," the grocer added, taking the money.

"Well, then, have a good night. I'll be back when I can." John ruffled their son's hair and started down the stairs with the family calling out their thanks and good wishes to him.

One more such visit to the owner of a secondhand store where many residents of the neighborhood bought their clothes, and finally he made a quick visit to the local parish church. The vicar there would distribute money directly to the people who needed it most. John's pockets were nearly empty as he headed home, but his mind was content.

Chapter Three

~May 13~

There were very few diamonds John didn't like, but what society called a "diamond of the first water" was one. He had no time or patience for the diamonds of society, not after what two of them had done to his sister when she had made her debut. No, his only interest in society now was the diamonds he could steal from the wealthy ladies who dripped with them and hardly noticed when one or two went missing, and he only liked the stones for the money they brought which allowed him to help the poor.

And yet it was a diamond who grabbed his attention this evening as she held court in the middle of a bevy of dandified suitors. His natural inclination and her brilliant charisma drew him to her, and at the moment, it was more than he could resist.

A burst of laughter drew him into her web of admirers. What in the world could this young woman be talking about that enthralled so many gentlemen? He couldn't have moved away even if he'd tried.

"Have you *seen* Lord Macomb's newest stallion? I declare, no horse that large should be allowed on Rotten Row at the height of the promenade, and then there was this child holding his reins!" she said with a broad smile on her full, pink lips.

"How old was the boy?" someone called out.

"He couldn't have been above five or six, and hardly stood taller than the horse's knees!" she answered with a giggle.

The group of men burst out laughing again. John was horrified that such a small child would be left to care for a horse of that size and strength.

"What did *you* do, Miss Sheffield?" another gentleman asked.

"Me? Oh, I stayed a few feet away—far enough so the child couldn't see me, but close enough in case assistance was required," the girl said.

John nodded approvingly but managed to keep his mouth shut. He shouldn't even be here listening to her. He wasn't here to enjoy the party, he reminded himself, and he was here to do a job. He should simply move off, but something kept him rooted right where he stood.

"Did Macomb come back when he said he would?" someone asked.

"No! He came back a full ten minutes later, and when he did, he started to hand the boy tuppence. The child stopped him from retrieving the reins and held out his little hand and said, 'That'll be five pence and a farthing, if you would, my lord.'"

The men all burst out laughing again, and even John had a hard time keeping a smile from twitching onto his lips.

"Macomb began to argue with the child," Miss Sheffield continued, "but the boy stood firm. His lordship had promised him a tuppence for ten minutes, but he'd been gone for well over twenty. The child wanted his due!"

"Did he pay the boy?" John asked despite himself. The young woman blinked her lovely deep-green eyes at him before a smile lit her face. "Of course, once I had caught his lordship's eye and let him know that he had to do so."

"With just a look?" John asked.

"Oh, I can convey a great deal of meaning with a look, my lord," Miss Sheffield said.

The gentlemen around her once again exploded with laughter.

"Indeed, Miss Sheffield, you could slay me with one glance of those beautiful eyes," a man said, placing his hands over his heart.

"And I!" another piped in.

"I could only hope to be spared such a look," a third gentleman said, reaching out an imploring hand in her direction.

The girl laughed. "Oh, gentlemen, you should be on the stage. I would come to see you all every night."

John laughed and shook his head before moving off to scout for the sort of diamonds he'd originally come for.

~*~

When Lydia had finished regaling the gentlemen with her story, they all drifted away except for a few lingerers. She excused herself, however, and went in search of the gentleman who'd joined the group late.

He was the same man who she'd seen a few nights ago at Lady Kershaw's ball, she was certain of it. He was the man in the gray coat who'd stolen the diamonds!

How had she never noticed the gentleman before? Somehow, he hadn't come to her attention before this, although it was true she hadn't been in town for very long. She'd been sure she'd met every eligible gentleman, and even a number of whom were not so eligible but wished they were.

She gave a little laugh at that thought and strolled deliberately through Lady Emmerton's drawing room looking for him.

"Good evening, Miss Sheffield," Lady Sorrell said, forcing Lydia to stop.

"Oh, good evening."

"You seem to be looking for someone. Perhaps I can help?" asked her friend and fellow member of the Lady's Wagering Whist Society. Joining that elite group of ladies had definitely been the smartest move Lydia had made since coming to London. With it, she immediately gained seven very good friends, nearly all of them older and wiser than she. Only one other woman was new to society like herself, and Lydia had quickly made fast friends with her. It was so wonderful being with someone as forthright and clear-headed as Diana Hemshawe.

"Thank you. There was a man in a dark blue coat who was part of a group of gentlemen I was speaking with, but he disappeared before I could ask for an introduction."

"What did he look like?" her friend asked.

"Rather ordinary, actually. Dark blond hair, brown intelligent-looking eyes," Lydia answered, still looking around.

"He sounds exactly like the sort of gentleman your father would be happy to see you with," Lady Sorrell answered with a little laugh.

Lydia turned back to her friend, giggling. "You're right. I'm certain he is. Papa would be so happy if I married someone who was as clever as he."

"Well, lets see if we can't find your mystery man," Lady Sorrell said, tucking her hand into Lydia's elbow.

They proceeded to promenade about the rooms, but it seemed as if the fellow had just disappeared!

~May 14~

"Did you see Tina driving through the park yesterday with my nephew?" Mrs. Aldridge gushed the moment she walked into Lady Norman's game room the following day.

Many of the ladies were already assembled for the weekly meeting of the Ladies Wagering Whist Society and having a cup of tea before they all sat down to play cards.

"Who *hasn't* seen them?" the Duchess of Kendall asked, depressing Mrs. Aldridge's excitement quite effectively.

Lydia felt bad for Mrs. Aldridge. She was trying so hard to fit into a very well-established society. It wasn't her fault her husband was in manufacturing. She was doing all she could to better the family's social standing and provide opportunities for her son who, Lydia understood, was quite a catch in the marriage mart.

She, herself, wasn't interested in marrying for money—not that her father was wealthy. As the third son of a marquess, he had had to work for most of his adult life, much like Mr. Aldridge, but at least she was not being compelled to find a rich husband. There were a number of girls her age who were, and therefore looking quite closely at the younger Mr. Aldridge when he actually attended society functions, which he didn't do quite as often as Mrs. Aldridge wished. The family did have the benefit of being related to Lord Ainsby, who was an earl and the nephew under discussion at the moment.

The duchess, however, felt it was her job to keep the *mushroom*—the duchess's word, not Lydia's—in her place. Clashes between the two ladies were, sadly, growing each time they met. Luckily, things hadn't come to a head yet, and Lady Norman or Lady Blakemore always managed to keep the women at different card tables so they wouldn't have to spend too much time in each other's company.

One thing the duchess absolutely hated about Mrs. Aldridge, which Lydia happened to adore, was her sweet little Cavalier King Charles Spaniel, which she brought with her nearly everywhere she went. Mrs. Aldridge's husband had named the dog Duchess, which annoyed the Duchess of Kendall to no end. Lydia thought it was immensely amusing. She wondered at anyone who could not love such a sweet-tempered, adoring little pup!

Lydia reached down and scratched the dog in question, which was sitting expectantly next to her owner, behind her long, floppy black ears and got her hand licked in appreciation. "Haven't they been seen together a number of times already?" Lydia asked.

"Three times in just this past week," Mrs. Aldridge gushed.

"My word!" Lady Norman said. Since Tina was her daughter, Lydia was rather surprised she wasn't aware of how many times they'd been out. "I wonder if I should have a word with her. Being seen so often with just one gentleman could make people talk."

Chapter Four

"**O**h, I think we're past that," Diana said to Lady Norman with a little laugh. "I've heard talk from the races I've attended as well at parties." She bent down to help herself to a lemon tart from the plate on a low table. She then picked up the entire plate and moved it to a higher spot where the dog couldn't get at the treats.

"Does your father know you attend so many races?" Lady Moreton asked the girl.

Diana gave a little giggle around her mouthful of tart and had to make use of her handkerchief. After she swallowed she said, "My father is always with me, my lady."

"Oh." Lady Moreton gave her a little smile, but she clearly was confused by a father who took his daughter to horse races. Lydia understood he not only took her but, in fact, encouraged her to ride in them! It was quite scandalous! Lydia loved it.

"I've had an unusual occurrence," Lydia said, during a momentary lull in the conversation. She hadn't intended to discuss the mystery gentleman she'd seen twice now, but somehow the comment just popped out of her mouth unbidden.

"Oh?" Lady Sorrell asked, turning toward her along with a number of the other ladies.

"As Lady Sorrell is well aware, there's a gentleman I've seen twice now who I've never met. I have tried to be introduced to him, but he seems to keep disappearing on me," she said with a little laugh.

"How could it be there is a gentleman who *you* haven't met, Lydia?" Diana asked with a broad smile on her face. "I was certain every eligible man has made himself known to you."

Lydia laughed out loud. "And a number of those who aren't so eligible," she added.

"How is it that you have met so many?" Lady Moreton asked. She seemed to be honestly curious.

"I don't know, to be honest. I don't have a great fortune—well, none at all to be strictly truthful. But somehow..." Lydia didn't quite know how to finish her sentence because she didn't have an answer.

"It's your sweet temper and charm," Lady Norman said without hesitation. "Everyone loves a girl who laughs."

Lydia giggled. "You are too kind, my lady."

"No, just honest," the woman said.

"And correct," Lady Blakemore said. "More girls should follow your lead, Miss Sheffield. You are always a pleasure to speak with. Deferential to your elders and, as Lady Norman says, always laughing about something. Quite charming!"

Lydia could feel her face heat with such effusive praise. "You are too kind! But as I say, there is clearly one gentleman who not only doesn't wish to meet me but seems to be *deliberately* avoiding me. Do you remember when I pointed him out to you last week, Lady Norman? The man in the gray coat?"

"I do remember you trying to point him out to me, but I never saw him. He'd left the room by the time I looked," the woman said, thankfully not mentioning the fact that Lydia had accused him of removing some pins from a lady's hair.

"Yes. I saw him again later that evening, but once again, he escaped before I could approach him. And then last night he even spoke to me when I was telling a story to some gentlemen, but then when my story was finished and I wanted to make his acquaintance, he was gone once again! It is the most frustrating thing!" Lydia said. She had to laugh about it; otherwise, she might have wanted to grind her teeth in annoyance.

"Well, since none of us have seen him, how could we possibly tell you who it is you've been seeing?" the duchess asked.

"I don't know. Perhaps there is someone new in Town? A gentleman of about average height with dark blond hair and brown eyes?" Lydia asked.

"He sounds as if he could be any one of a number of gentlemen. Does he dress particularly well or particularly badly?" Lady Moreton asked.

"No. I mean, he dresses in a very elegant but understated way, so nothing that would stand out," Lydia said with a shrug.

"Then you'll simply need to point him out to us the next time you see him," Lady Blakemore said.

"Yes. I suppose I will," Lydia agreed. "Thank you."

It was very unsatisfying, but there didn't seem to be any way around it. She may never know who this mystery man was. She supposed she should simply figure out a way to get him out of her mind. Easier said than done.

~May 15~

John took a peek at the cards that had just been dealt to him by the dealer at Powell's Club. Gambling was his one vice—or so he told himself. At least he wasn't addicted like so many other gentlemen of the ton.

No, John knew when to stop, which was a good thing because he simply didn't have the funds to lose. Every penny he could spare went to the good people of the Rookeries. He did, however, set aside a few pounds from those Mr. Meir gave him for his own gambling pleasure. If his luck held and they grew in number, he always gave the lot of it away to those who truly needed it.

Tonight he'd almost walked away when the pile of chips in front of him had dwindled. But the most interesting conversation kept him rooted to his chair.

"Are you certain it was Emmerton who you saw?" Lord Hanslow said, tapping the table with his cards. He did it every time he had a terrible hand.

"Absolutely," the Viscount Swindon said, with a very pleased grin on his face. He had a good hand, John thought, either that or he was also aware of Hanslow's habit of tapping his cards. "I even stopped and had a word with him after he left the establishment."

"You didn't!" Hanslow said.

"I did. And he showed me a lovely diamond set he'd just purchased," Swindon added.

"A congé?" Hanslow asked. "That's an awfully expensive way to cut loose a mistress. I would have gone with rubies or something else not quite as expensive."

Swindon just laughed. "When the lady in question is the incomparable Maria—"

"A true diamond herself," Hanslow said on a sigh. "So, she is finally going to be free to seek pleasures elsewhere."

"Indeed, she is," Swindon practically giggled.

"You don't have your eye trained on her now, do you?" Hanslow asked carefully.

"Gentlemen, are you going to gossip or play the damn game?" Lord Meriton asked.

John could only chuckle at the man's impatience. Swindon put down his cards, displaying a measly seven and a three. "I've got nothing. And yes, she's mine—or soon will be."

The dealer turned over all the cards on the table and declared John the winner. He was certain if Swindon had been paying more attention, he would have continued playing and probably could have won the hand. John didn't mind the distraction as he pulled the pile of chips toward himself. Not only did this tip his winnings to the positive side, he'd just gotten invaluable information.

Diamonds.

They were probably sitting in Lord Emmerton's safe at this very moment, waiting to be presented to his mistress before he sent her packing. A safe that John had discovered the location of only a few days earlier when he'd been at a soiree hosted by the lovely Lady Emmerton. Sadly, she didn't own any diamonds, or if she did, she didn't keep them in the safe in their study—he'd checked.

"You wouldn't happen to know when this lovely is going to be set free?" John asked nonchalantly.

"I believe he's seeing her tomorrow, which means that *I* will be seeing her on Saturday. Don't you get any ideas, Welles," Lord Swindon said, narrowing his eyes at John.

He gave a little shrug. "Well, if she's not interested, I do hope you will be kind enough to inform us." He gave Hanslow a wink.

The man chuckled. "Yes, Swindon, you don't know that—"

"I'm certain I can convince her," the man interrupted. "Now are we playing cards or gossiping like a group of old women?"

Chapter Five

John adjusted the old coat he'd just purchased from the secondhand clothing shop so it sat lopsided on his shoulders, furthering the look that the garment didn't really fit him. Satisfied with his appearance of an old coat, patched breeches, dirty stockings, and rough work shoes, he knocked on the service door at the home of Lord Emmerton.

He would have loved to see the face of that diamond now were she to see him this way. He nearly gave a laugh. A girl like that wouldn't even give him a second look.

It bothered him only a little that he was still thinking about Miss Sheffield. He didn't know what it was about her that had fixed his attention. Normally, he passed such people by without a second thought. Somehow, this one had not only caught him but stayed with him. He just couldn't shake that vision of her, surrounded by gentlemen, positively glowing with life and laughter as she told her silly story.

She had been absolutely captivating.

"Yes?" the voice of a maid shook him from his wandering mind.

He doffed his cap, doing his best imitation of his friends of the Rookeries, and said, "Afternoon, mum. I'm 'ere to check on t'chimbleys."

The young woman looked at him curiously. "On the chimneys? They were just cleaned the day before."

"Yes'm. I'm 'ere to make sure the werk were good 'nough. Sent over a new boy, we did, an' I wanna make sure he did a good 'nough job."

"Oh, I see. Just a moment and I'll call the housekeeper, Mrs. Scott." The maid closed the door in his face.

John took a step back and waited nearly twenty minutes for the housekeeper to arrive. When she did, he explained his purpose once again. She gave a satisfied nod, accepting his story, and then started to lead him into the house.

She paused just inside the door. "Are your shoes clean?"

"Yes, mum." He lifted his shoes and showed her the soles, one nearly worn all the way through. She gave a small tsk, but continued on into the kitchens and from there into the main part of the house.

"He cleaned the one in the mistress' room," she began.

"Er... Ye sure about that, mum? I believe it was 'is lordship's room where 'e began," John said as politely as he could.

She paused to look back at him and then nodded. "Oh, yes, you are correct. It was the master's chamber where he began."

John had been prepared for such a test and had quizzed the boy in question thoroughly before coming. He followed the housekeeper up the stairs.

After a great show of inspecting the chimney in his lordship's chamber while the housekeeper looked on, he gave a satisfied nod. "If ye wouldn't mind, I'll just check one more in the study," he said, wiping his dirty hands on his breeches.

The housekeeper frowned at him but gave a nod and preceded him back down to the study. Instead of going directly to the fireplace as he had before, John stepped up to the window and looked out. The boy who'd cleaned these chimneys was sitting across the street in the park awaiting John's signal. Upon seeing him, the child stood and zipped across the street toward the house.

"The chimney, sir," the housekeeper reminded him. "I don't have all day for you to admire the view," she said sternly.

"Yes,'m. Beggin' yer pardon, mum," John said, doffing his cap again. He began his inspection of the chimney once again. As he was doing so, some noises and shouts could be heard emanating from the back of the house.

"What in the world..." the housekeeper began.

John popped out from the chimney to see a different maid come in, bobbing a curtsy to the housekeeper. "I beg your pardon, Mrs. Scott, but your presence is required in the kitchen."

The woman gave a curt nod. "You will finish up here quickly, do you hear?"

"Yes'm," John said. He watched as the woman hurried from the room, closing the door behind her.

He immediately wiped his hands on the clean handkerchief in his pocket. A pin came out of another, and within moments, he was picking the lock on the cabinet standing against the wall opposite the door. It was a beautiful piece that John had admired the last time he'd been in the house for

Lady Emmerton's soiree. A vision of the diamond telling her tale briefly swam in his mind's eye, but he didn't have time for such dreaming. He didn't know how long he had before the housekeeper came back.

The lock opened, allowing a desk to drop down. Behind it was a plain piece of wood, which if one didn't know better, would look like nothing more than the back of the cabinet. A hidden keyhole was revealed however in the lower left-hand corner. This one was even easier to pick, and within moments, he'd swung open the hidden door to reveal the family's safe.

When he'd checked the contents of it during the soiree, it had held only a few pieces of jewelry—emeralds, rubies, and pearls, and some papers which interested John not at all. Today, however, a lovely new blue box sat just in front. He was just reaching for it when he heard someone clearing their throat.

He spun around, certain that very soon he would be seeing nothing but the inside of the city goal.

He could barely believe his eyes. It was the diamond. Not the necklace he'd been about to admire, but the young lady who he hadn't been able to get out of his mind. For a moment, he was certain his eyes were playing a cruel trick on him.

~May 16~

Lydia had never been so happy to turn a conversation to Shakespeare. She appreciated the bard's work, but preferred the ancient Greek playwrights. However, as the conversation at Lady Emmerton's at-home had been leaning toward tearing apart another young lady who was also making her debut, Lydia decided she much preferred the topic of Shakespeare.

"I just couldn't believe the gown Miss Pensley wore to the theatre last night," Lady Pendleton said during a slight lull in the conversation. "It was so low as to be almost indecent!"

"Certainly not appropriate for one so young," Lady Emmerton agreed.

"What play did you see, my lady?" Lydia asked, deliberately turning the direction of the conversation.

"Oh, I don't remember," Lady Pendleton said, with a dismissive wave of her hand. "Who actually pays attention to what's on the stage?"

"It was A Midsummer Night's Dream," Lady Emmerton said.

"Oh, I do so love the comedies," Lydia said. "I must say I haven't read that one in a while."

"*Have* you read them?" Lady Pendleton asked with some surprise in her voice.

"Of course! Sadly, my father doesn't have copies of the plays here in Town, but we've got every one at our estate in Essex," Lydia said.

"Emmerton has them all as well. If you'd like to borrow one, I'm certain he wouldn't mind," their hostess offered.

Lydia jumped at the chance to escape the room. "Oh, that is so very kind of you, my lady. If you don't mind, I believe I will."

"Of course, the study is just at the bottom of the stairs," the woman said. "I'll call a maid who can show you the way."

"I'm certain I can find it. If you'll excuse me for a moment, I'll just go and fetch it." Lydia gave the ladies a slight curtsy and then went off in search of a book she had absolutely no intention of reading.

To say she was shocked to catch a robbery in progress would be a vast understatement. She'd walked silently into the room to see a man who, despite his rough clothing, looked strangely familiar.

She watched him for a moment as he finished picking the lock on the safe, studying him and trying to recall where she'd seen him before. When he turned his profile slightly toward her, it hit her—this was her mysterious gentleman! Her gasp at this realization had him spinning around to face her.

Chapter Six

*L*ydia immediately held her hands up to stop him from saying anything. "I will not say a word if you close that back up immediately—without removing anything," she added, not certain that the stipulation wouldn't be obvious.

He did as she said, keeping one eye on the door as he relocked the safe, closed a hidden door, locked that, and then closed the desk.

He stood before her, his face serious and worried, as it should have been.

"I expect a full explanation of this," she informed him. She was about to say more when she heard footsteps approaching. "But not here and not now," she said quickly. "You may pick me up at my home tomorrow at three and take me for a drive through the park. Number ten, Carlton Street."

Just as the door opened, Lydia turned toward the bookshelf and pretended that she'd been studying the books for some time. She turned to see who'd entered the room. A woman who looked like she could only be the housekeeper stopped just inside the doorway.

"I beg your pardon, Miss," the woman started, clearly not sure who she was or what she was doing in the study.

"Oh, I'm Miss Sheffield. Lady Emmerton was kind enough to lend me a copy of one of Shakespeare's plays. I'm just looking for it," Lydia said.

"Yes, of course, Miss. I apologize for the chimney sweep," the woman said, indicating the thief who somehow managed to look as if he'd been in the chimney the whole time.

He scratched his cheek leaving a streak of soot with his fingers and then wiped his hands on his breeches. "All looks aright to me, mum. Thank ye, vera much fer allowin' me to check," he said in a voice higher than the one she'd heard the previous evening.

"You don't need to check the other one the boy cleaned?" the woman asked.

"No, mum. If'n he did two good, the rest should be fine," he said.

The housekeeper gave a nod of approval and then turned and left the room, clearly expecting the man to follow.

He gave the brim of his hat a wiggle in Lydia's direction before following the housekeeper out the door.

"At three, Miss Sheffield," he said under his breath in his natural voice before leaving the room.

~*~

"Did you meet anyone interesting at Lady Emmerton's this afternoon," Lydia's father asked after they had been served their dinner that evening.

Lydia put down her fork before taking the bite of food off of it. "Why do you ask?" He couldn't have heard that she'd met the thief. No one knew she'd done so except the Emmerton's housekeeper, and naturally she hadn't known who he was. She'd thought he was there inspecting the fireplaces or some such nonsense.

Her father smiled but narrowed his eyes a bit. "I was just curious. Making conversation."

"Oh!" Lydia gave a little giggle. "Of course. No. There was no one of interest there. I was hoping some of the gentlemen I'd met last evening at the soiree would be there paying their respects but no such luck." She popped her fork into her mouth.

"I have to admit, I was hoping the same thing," her father said with a chuckle of his own. "I heard you had quite the audience at one point. Emmerton himself came up to me in the card room and mentioned it."

Lydia laughed honestly. "Yes. I think I had at least six or seven gentlemen listening to a silly tale."

"You do know how to tell a good story," her father agreed. "So, who was there? Anyone interesting? Or anyone who you'd like to get to know better?"

"Papa," Lydia said, giving her father a look, "I am meeting plenty of gentlemen. You should be happy with that."

"I am! I am. But I was just wondering if there was anyone in particular who'd caught your attention." Her father gave her a wink over his glass of wine.

"Not as yet. I assure you, you'll be the first to know."

"Well, I should be! If any young man wants to court you, he needs to seek my permission first," he said, after taking a sip from his glass. "Not that I would say no to almost any gentleman you had an interest in."

"But you might to some?" she asked curiously.

"Well, yes, of course. I can't have you marrying just anyone."

"What are your qualifications?"

He paused to chew his food and think about his answer. "Well, he should be kind," he started. "And have an excellent sense of humor, but then again, any man who would be interested in you would since you are quite a funny one."

Lydia giggled at that.

"And he should be from a good family, naturally. It would be nice if he had money, but I won't make that a requirement, even though we're not exactly swimming in it either," he continued.

"So you *don't* think I should marry for money?" she clarified.

"No, sweetheart, I think you should marry for love, like your mother and I did," he said, his eyes growing misty as they always did whenever he mentioned her mother. It had been thirteen years since she'd died in childbirth, and both of them still felt the pain of her loss.

"Well, I'll let you know if I fall for anyone."

"I know you will. You won't be able to keep it to yourself." He laughed.

"Are you calling me a chatterbox, sir?" she said with mock-anger.

"No! I would never *call* you that."

She put down her fork and frowned at him before the both burst into laughter.

"Well, you'll be pleased to know that I did meet a gentleman at Lady Emmerton's today, and he will be taking me for a drive tomorrow afternoon in the park," Lydia admitted. She hadn't been entirely certain she'd wanted to tell her father about that, but since he was so concerned—as always!—she thought she should try to allay some of his worries.

"So there were gentlemen there!"

"Well, yes," she admitted. She hoped he wouldn't question others about who had been in attendance since there hadn't actually been any gentlemen paying proper calls on Lady Emmerton.

"What is his name?"

It was the most natural question, but it stopped Lydia cold. She had no idea! He hadn't told her! She'd made sure to tell him hers, but he hadn't reciprocated. Well, he hadn't exactly been in a position to do so, but still... It was going to be awkward not knowing.

"I don't remember!" she said, playing on her shock that she truly didn't know. "I'm sure someone must have said it, but I can't recall. Isn't that funny?"

"So you are going driving with a gentleman whose name you don't know?" Her father became quite serious all of a sudden.

"Yes. I'll have to somehow be clever and get him to tell me without letting on that I can't remember. Maybe we'll see someone who knows him and they'll call out a greeting. You know the park is always so crowded in the afternoons."

"Hmm, I don't know if I like that, Lydia," her father said.

"Oh, it'll be fine. We are going to be in a very public place at the most crowded time of day, Papa. Nothing could possibly happen," Lydia chided him.

"And you will take your maid," her father reminded her.

"I don't know that they'll be room for her in his carriage, but I'll send her to the park to await me should I feel at all uncomfortable in the gentleman's presence. Would that make you feel better?"

Her father truly frowned at her. "I don't like it. You should at the very least know the name of the gentleman."

"I know, Papa, and it's very silly of me to have forgotten it. I must not have been paying attention when we were introduced. But he is a gentleman, I'm absolutely certain of that. And I'm pretty certain he's a peer—he *was* at Lady Emmerton's soiree last night. And, oh, I've seen him plenty of times at various parties, I assure you."

"But you don't know his name."

"No, isn't that funny? Well, I'll be sure to tell you what it is tomorrow night, how's that?"

He slowly nodded. "I suppose that will have to do for now. But do have your maid at the park, should anything happen."

"At the height of the afternoon promenade," she said teasingly.

This time he clearly didn't find her levity amusing.

Chapter Seven

The entire night Lydia tossed and turned and wondered just how incredibly stupid and foolhardy she'd been in Lord Emmerton's library. Going out driving with a complete stranger! And one who was a thief?

Would her reputation survive it?

At least she'd had the good sense to ensure they would be surrounded by other people as they would be out at the height of the promenade. Should he even attempt to do anything untoward, she had recourse and did have the foresight to tell her maid to wait for her by the gate to the park. She could join her there either before or after the drive, or even in the middle should it become necessary. Lydia sincerely hoped it would not, but it was always good to be prepared.

She was still pacing and worrying when she heard the bell ring at the front door. She stopped to look at the clock. She was glad she'd gotten ready early.

Before the footman could even answer the door, she was walking toward it.

Oh, my goodness, she nearly groaned as her nerves started to overtake her. She paused for a moment. No, she could do this. It would be fine. She straightened her back and continued to the door.

"Miss Lydia, I'll answer that," their footman said, trotting up from behind her.

"It's all right, Michael. I know who it is. If anyone asks, I've gone out for a drive in the park and will be back in an hour or so."

"But—"

She popped out the door before she could hear anything further and closed it firmly behind her.

"You're early," she said, allowing the gentleman to help her up into his phaeton. It was a fine vehicle and looked, if not new, then at least in very good shape. So far so good. Although, if he really was a thief, then she supposed he had the funds for anything.

"My apologies," he said, climbing up behind her. "I thought it would be better to be early than late."

She didn't say anything as she scooted over on the seat so he could take up the reins next to her.

After they reached the park and entered the flow of traffic slowly making its way around, she turned to him. "I'm afraid you have the advantage of me, sir."

"I beg your pardon? I should think it would be the other way around, Miss Sheffield," he said with a slight smile.

"I don't know your name," she clarified.

"Oh! I apologize. John Welles, er, Viscount Welles," he said.

"You're a viscount? Then what were you doing with your hand in the Emmerton's safe?" Lydia asked rather shocked. "Or is your estate so impoverished that that's what you've been reduced to—although if it is true, the normal way of things is to marry well, not resort to thievery."

Viscount Welles did laugh at that. "Yes. I am aware. It wasn't for me that I was stealing."

"Oh?"

"There are a number of businesses, as well as individuals, who I support," he said. "I just don't, er, have the necessary funds of my own to do so."

"I don't understand."

"They're located in an area of town called the Rookeries. St. Giles? Surely, you've heard of it?"

"Of course I've heard of it!" She was tempted to scowl at the man for thinking her such an idiot, but instead she laughed. "I am very well aware of the poorer sections of Town, although I have to admit, I've not visited them myself."

"No, of course not," he said under his breath.

"You don't even know me and yet you presume a great deal, sir," Lydia said, feeling a burning anger beginning to grow in the pit of her stomach. She never got angry! How dare this man force feelings on her she didn't like.

"I know your sort," he said dismissively.

She turned toward him, forcing a polite smile onto her lips. "Oh, really? And pray tell, what sort is that?"

"Always surrounded by adoring men. You are beautiful, admired—what society calls a diamond of the first water." He sneered.

She burst out laughing. She couldn't help it. His contempt for her was abundantly evident. "What is it? Jealousy? Or do you simply believe you are better than those of us who actually enjoy being a part of society?"

"Jealous? Of what? Of the men you've got eating out of the palm of your hand? Hardly!"

So he *was* jealous. But of the men he referenced or her? "How is it that I've not seen you at many parties, my lord?"

He frowned and focused on his driving once again. "I don't care for such empty amusements."

Ah, so it was of her ability to move easily through society that he was jealous. "What *do* you care for? Stealing? Helping the poor? Anything else?"

He pursed his lips together. "Nothing you would understand, I'm sure."

"Right. Because I'm a stupid little girl," she said, nodding. The fire within her belly grew hotter.

"You are most certainly not a little girl, but no, I do not believe one such as you would be able to understand anything that interests me—and that includes caring for the poor and my other private pursuits."

Lydia could only shake her head sadly at this man's narrow-minded stupidity. He knew absolutely nothing about her—not the hours she spent every single day teaching the poor children of the miners in the town close to her father's estate, nor did he have any idea of her own academic prowess. All he saw was a pretty face and a socially adept young lady and thought the worst of her. "How sad."

"What, that you couldn't comprehend my interests?"

"No. That you cannot understand what an imbecile you are," she said.

His face turned bright red, but he didn't once take his eyes from the crowded path before them.

Lydia too turned to watch the passing carriages. She spotted Lady Norman's daughter, Tina, out driving with Lord Ainsby. She remembered the ladies of the Whist Society discussing how often Tina had been out with that particularly gentleman, but this was the first time she'd actually seen them.

"Oh, do pull up a moment," Lydia said. "I see a friend of mine." She caught Tina's eye and waved.

As the two carriages pulled abreast of one another, they both paused.

"Good afternoon, Tina," Lydia called out. "You are look as dashing as ever, Lord Ainsby!" she said with a giggle. It felt good to turn her attention away from the unpleasantness that was Lord Welles. Sadly, she couldn't completely ignore the man. Politeness decreed that she at least introduce him to her friends.

"Good afternoon, Lydia!" Tina said happily.

"Miss Sheffield, it is an honor as always," her companion said.

"May I present Lord Welles?" Lydia said, indicating the gentleman sitting next to her. "Miss Ayres and Lord Ainsby."

"Very pleased," Lord Ainsby said. "I believe we've played a hand or two at Powell's, have we not?"

"Yes, I believe so," Lord Welles said, giving them both a polite nod.

Someone called out from behind them.

"Ah, I believe that is our cue to move on," Lord Ainsby said with a laugh. "Ta-ta!"

Silence reigned for a few minutes as Lord Welles managed his horse.

"Miss Sheffield are you going to turn me in to the authorities?" he asked after a few minutes.

"You have immunity, my lord, merely based on the fact that you are a peer of the realm. I can make your activities know to the *ton* and ruin your reputation, but you probably don't give a fig about that," Lydia answered with honesty.

He nodded. "You are correct on both counts."

"However, I can ensure you are not welcome at any other social function ever again. If you have any family, you can be sure they will be persona non grata as well should I make your activities public knowledge. And then, there is the small matter of the fact that my father is a well-respected lawyer, the son of a marquess, and very well respected throughout the government."

"What do you want?" he ground out from between his teeth.

She put her hand to her chin and thought about it. "I don't know as yet. You know us diamonds of society. Such silly creatures we are. We have trouble making up our minds, possibly even thinking at all. I will need some time to consider it."

He gave a little laugh. "Touché."

"You may pull up there, by the gate, my lord. My maid is waiting for me," Lydia said, once again happy she'd had the foresight to have Polly there in case she had had enough of this man's company before he was able to return her home.

She certainly had no desire to spend another quarter of an hour with him while he saw her back to her door—a more infuriating gentleman she didn't think she'd ever met. She was beginning to wonder just what it was that had so captivated her before. Ah right, he hadn't actually spoken to her so she'd had no idea what a horrid, narrow-minded creature he was.

~May 17~

As always, John went straight to his mother's private drawing room as soon as he got home. And then, as he'd done for the past month or more, he remembered she wouldn't be there but in her bed.

A terrible bout of influenza had stolen all of the energy from her, and she'd hardly been able to stir from her bed ever since. Every night he prayed she would get better, but with each passing day, he worried more and more she would end her days sooner rather than later.

"Good afternoon, Mother," he started to say before he had even fully entered her bedchamber. He stopped when he noticed her bed was empty.

A giggle caught his attention. "I'm over here, John," she said from a chair that had been pushed right up next to the fireplace. Despite the growing warmth of spring, a fire crackled merrily next to her. She was in her night rail with a blanket covering her legs and a shawl draped across her shoulders.

"Mother! What are you doing out of bed?" he scolded.

"Ugh! I couldn't stand being there for another moment," she complained. "And besides, I was feeling much better today, so I thought sitting up for some time by the fire would be pleasant."

"But are you warm enough? How are you feeling?" he asked, coming to kneel by her side.

She caressed a hand across his head. "I've got a hot brick under my feet and if this fire was any hotter, I would be throwing off my shawl. I'm half-tempted to do so anyway."

"No!" He adjusted it higher on her shoulders so it caressed her neck. "It's wonderful you're feeling so strong. Truly! But I don't want you to strain yourself. How long have you been sitting here?"

"Just for the past quarter of an hour. I'm perfectly fine. Now, tell me what you've been up to," she said, smiling down at him.

CHAPTER EIGHT

John sighed and relented with his cosseting. He got up and sat in the chair opposite her and a little farther away from the fire, which was much too hot for him. "You will be happy to hear I was taking a young lady for a drive in the park," he told her. He didn't hide anything from his mother—she knew all about everything he did. Truly, everything.

"Oh, really?" she said, her eyes lighting up, either that or her fever was returning.

He gave a little sigh and then laughed. "You know I went to Lord Emmerton's yesterday to, er, relieve him of a certain diamond necklace he'd bought for his mistress?"

"Yes, you did mention you were going to do that. Hopefully, that will satisfy Mr. Meir so he can return to Amsterdam and leave you alone for a while."

He smiled. His mother didn't like Mr. Meir very much, but she understood the necessity of continuing with the connection. "Yes, well, I just reached into the safe when a young lady walked into the room. I had my back to the door, so I didn't see her right away."

"Oh, no! What did you do?" Her hand flew to her mouth and her eyes went wide.

"I didn't know what to do, but she said she wouldn't tell anyone if I took her for a drive today," he said.

"Ah, well that's rather clever."

He just gave a little shrug. He wasn't sure what to think of it.

"And will she keep quiet? Did you explain to her what you were doing and why?"

He shook his head. "She's a society miss, what does she know of poverty and the Rookeries? I tried to explain it to her, but she just narrowed her eyes and didn't seem to understand what I was saying."

"Oh, dear. So much for her being clever."

"I'm certain she's going to want something. I asked her straight out what it might be, but she said she didn't know yet. It was clear she was thinking of letting it be known what I've been doing. I can only hope she's able to hold her tongue and not go gossiping to all of her friends and her mother, who would probably spread the word even further." John shook his head in disgust thinking about the gossiping women of the ton.

"But what might she want in exchange for her silence?" his mother asked, beginning to wring her hands.

"I don't know." He reached out and stilled them with his own. They were cold, which worried him. "I'm sure I'll find out soon enough, and when I do, I'll know what to do."

"*Why* must you do this, John? You know full well that you would not have to resort to illegal means to support the people of the Rookeries if you just did as your father and marry someone of wealth."

John gave a disbelieving laugh. "Yes, and you know where that landed him. Broke. I'm still trying to fix all the damage he did to the estate, trying to pull as much money from it as he could."

"It's true I didn't have as much as he wished…"

"No, Mother, marrying a wealthy woman I have no interest in is not the answer."

"Your father and I—"

"Yes, your relationship was well enough, but if I ever marry—which I probably won't—it will be for love just like Louise did."

His mother sighed happily. "We were ever so lucky you introduced Mark to your sister. It was as if they were made for each other."

"I know," he smiled. "It was truly amazing and wonderful. And I don't think it's too much to ask that I be given the same opportunity."

"No, it's not," his mother said, reaching out to him.

He took her hand again and was abruptly reminded of how cold she was.

"Maybe someday I will have the opportunity to find the right girl for me, but what I want right now is for you to get back into bed. Come now, shall I carry you, or can you walk?" He stood and put his hands out for her to take, so he could help her from her chair.

"I would much rather stay right where I am," she started.

"I'm sure you would, but you've been out of bed for too long already. I don't want you to relapse. Come on now, be good," he coaxed her. "Shall I carry you?"

"No, no. I'll walk." She admitted defeat and allowed him to help her up and back to bed. She weighed next to nothing and was so frail, it truly frightened him.

~May 18~

Lydia was thoroughly enjoying her discussion with Lady Sorrell on the merits of Greek theatre over that of the early seventeenth century. Lady Crowther's soiree would have been deadly dull without Lady Sorrell and her intelligent discussions. Lydia had enjoyed them before this evening as well, and it always made ordinary parties so much more fun when the only other topic of conversation was who did what with whom. At home, she and her father regularly engaged in intellectual debate. Since coming to Town, however, she'd been so focused on the pretense of finding a husband that it was only at such gatherings, and when Lady Sorrell was present, she got to expand her mind at all.

"But how can you even compare Shakespeare to Sophocles? The style of the plays, the historical context... The differences are simply too vast," Lady Sorrell argued.

"But that is it, precisely. For two playwrights who are both best known for their tragedies..." Lydia caught sight of Viscount Welles over Lady Sorrell's shoulder. He was approaching them and would be within hearing distance within seconds.

She stuttered to a halt and then completely lost her train of thought. It didn't matter; he was nearly upon them. "...and then she put her hand into his as if she'd been meaning to dance with him after all!" she finished as the viscount stopped just next to a very confused-looking Lady Sorrell. "Oh, Viscount Welles, what a lovely surprise to see you here this evening," she said, her voice rising in pitch, although she had no idea why.

Her friend spun toward the gentleman, her mouth dropping open slightly.

"Have you met my friend, Lady Sorrell? My lady, the Viscount Welles," Lydia said, completing the introduction.

They acknowledged each other politely, but for some reason Lydia just couldn't stop talking. "We were just discussing Lady Martensen's ball, weren't we Lady Sorrell?"

The lady frowned at her. "Sophocles—"

"That would be Lord Martensen's new horse," Lydia interrupted. "His lordship was going on and on about the animal. It was the most boring thing you could possibly imagine." She gave a forced giggle.

"I believe I can—imagine how boring, that is," Lord Welles said, trying to keep a polite smile on his face. Lydia could see the effort in his eyes, which were already shifting away.

Lydia laughed as if he'd made the funniest joke. Thankfully, Lady Sorrell managed to put a smile, if a slightly confused one, on her lips.

"I don't suppose you've given any further thought to what we were discussing yesterday?" he asked.

Lydia had tried to come up with something, but truly she hadn't been able to think of anything he might be able to do for her. He couldn't further her position in society—he had almost none of his own. She didn't want money—not that he had any, clearly, if he had to steal so that he could support the poor. What else might one want from a gentleman?

Sadly, she shook her head. "Not as yet. I'll be sure to let you know." A thought occurred to her. "You aren't here to continue with your, er, hobby, are you?"

"I don't believe that is any of your concern," he answered, his voice curt and unpleasant.

"I beg to differ," she argued.

"What sort of hobby do you have, Lord Welles?" Lady Sorrell asked.

He gave Lydia a quick frown before pasting a polite smile onto his face as he turned to the lady. "I enjoy playing cards, my lady. Whist, vingt-et-un, that sort of thing."

"Oh, of course," she smiled. "Miss Sheffield and I are members of the Lady's Wagering Whist Society. We get together every week to play. I completely understand your passion for it."

"Really? A lady's whist club. How interesting," he said politely.

"We must discuss strategy sometime, my lord," Lydia said airily. "Perhaps you can give me some pointers. I have the hardest time trying to keep everything straight in my head, you know." She gave a little giggle just for effect.

He gave her a side-look as if he were trying to figure her out. "Indeed. I would be happy to do so. For now, however, you will excuse me while I go in search of the card room. And I shall leave you ladies to your gossip." He bowed and turned away.

"What in the world was that?" Lady Sorrell asked the moment he was out of earshot.

"I'm so sorry. He thinks I'm a featherbrained society miss. I just can't help perpetuating his misconception," Lydia admitted.

Her friend looked at her curiously. "Some young ladies would do all they could to disabuse a gentleman of that idea. Why are you not doing so?"

Lydia sighed. "I don't know. It just made me so angry when he assumed I was stupid and now..."

How could she explain to her friend that it frightened her to know that he may begin to like her were he to discover the truth? She had yet to decide what she thought of him, aside from anger at his baseless, biased assumption of her intelligence. But there was something about him... She so wanted to hate his condescension, but each time they met, she felt a twinge of attraction which made absolutely no sense to her. She wasn't yet ready to have him become one of her admirers. No, having him think so little of her was just fine—for now.

Chapter Nine

John wasn't ready to reassess his original opinion of Miss Sheffield's intelligence, but if she played whist, maybe she wasn't the complete idiot he thought her. He also had a sneaking suspicion that what she'd said to her friend just after he'd walked up to them was not on the same topic as they'd been discussing before he'd joined them.

Two things led him to this conclusion: one, Lady Sorrell's extremely confused expression; and two, as he'd walked up to her he thought he'd heard her say something about playwrights who wrote tragedies. The minute she'd spotted him, however, she switched to some inanity about someone dancing.

But why would a society miss be talking about playwrights? Unless she'd been speaking about a play she'd recently seen. One or another of Shakespeare's plays always seemed to be featured at the theatre. Yes, that must have been it. But why wouldn't she want him to know she'd been to the theatre?

It didn't make any sense to him. He turned and looked back at her but then had to take a second look. She was surrounded by men!

He'd only turned his back on her less than five minutes ago. How did she do that?

He went a little closer to observe. Two of the men were bantering back and forth about some sort of wager.

"I told Throck he was absolutely dead wrong," one of the dandies was saying while Miss Sheffield stood there giggling.

"Bet him a monkey!" another one of the gentlemen added in.

Miss Sheffield gasped, her eyes going wide. My goodness, but she was beautiful, John thought. He simply could not look away from her. She was positively glowing with... What was it? Joy? Happiness? Whatever it was, it was the same thing that had caught him the last time he'd seen her surrounded by men at Lady Emmerton's soiree. It was enthralling.

It was why she was always surrounded by men. She positively enthralled them with her...her beauty, her charm, her wit... John didn't quite know what it was, but it was definitely like a magnet for men, and he was as well caught as anyone else.

He pulled himself away. It wasn't easy, but he was not going to allow himself to get ensnared like those brainless twits. No, he had much more important things to do, and besides, he no longer enjoyed being in company as he once did—or so he told himself. He much preferred his solitude, his books, and his intellectual pursuits, not hanging on every word spoken by a beautiful, empty-headed young lady.

Yes, he had a job to do and people who were relying on him. Since Miss Sheffield had stopped his previous attempts at getting another piece for Mr. Meir, he was behind on his acquisitions.

He slipped up to the first floor where he was certain he would find Lady Crowther's bedchamber.

He had seen her wearing a beautiful diamond bracelet and earrings the other night, and she wasn't wearing them now. Hopefully they were still in her room and had not yet been returned to a safer place.

The third door he opened revealed what was most certainly the lady's chamber. Pale green silk covered the walls and a mass of lace-covered pillows decorated the large tester bed. A low fire burned in the grate, giving off just enough light for him to locate her dressing table. Sadly, there didn't seem to be any jewelry boxes just sitting out in plain sight.

He quickly glanced through the two drawers on either side of the table, but there was nothing there but odd pins, a hair brush, comb, and other accoutrements of a lady's toilet. There was no wardrobe in evidence, but there were two doors in the far wall. One must lead to the master's chamber and the other, perhaps, to the lady's dressing room?

He tried the door closer to the back wall. Success!

He lit the nub of a candle he'd brought with him from the fire and then went to examine the room. Built into the walls of the room were drawers and cabinets. He was certain he didn't have a lot of time, so he made a quick survey of the cabinets. The first was filled with Lady Crowther's underthings. But luck was with him as he discovered a jewelry box just inside the second cabinet he opened.

The diamonds were there but not for long. John replaced them with a playing card—the jack of diamonds—before ensuring that everything was otherwise exactly as he had found it. He was just about to leave when he heard the quiet click of a door closing in the lady's chamber. He peeked out to see a maid stoking up the fire and then helping herself to a glass of the brandy sitting on a side table next to a sofa in front of the fire. She plopped herself down to relax with her glass of stolen alcohol, sighing happily as she took a sip.

John needed to find another way out. He quietly closed the door he'd been peering out of and pressed his back to it. There had to be another door, a servant's entrance, but it was clearly well hidden among the cabinets. As quietly as he could, he opened and closed all of the taller cabinets toward the center of the room.

As he'd hoped, the third one was not a cabinet at all but led directly into the servants' stairs. He knew it would take him down to the kitchens where supper was being prepared, but there didn't seem to be any alternative. He'd managed to make it up the main stairs without being noticed. Hopefully he'd be able to do the same as he made his way through the kitchens.

"Can I help you, sir?" a maid asked as he popped out of the stairs. Damn! His luck seemed to have run out.

"Oh, no, thank you. I, er, seem to have lost my way," he said, pulling out his handkerchief and pretending to mop his face with it. He'd managed to cover all but his eyes when he said, "Ah! There's the door back to the party, is it?"

He immediately headed in that direction as the girl behind him said, "Yes sir, but..."

"Thank you," he called behind him. He slipped through the door and managed to disappear into the throng of partygoers within seconds. If she'd seen his face, it hadn't been for long. His clothing was deliberately nondescript, even ordinary for a member of the ton, so she wouldn't be able to mark him that way either. All he needed to do was escape the house without bumping into Miss Sheffield again. He had a strange suspicion she might know what he'd been doing just by looking at him.

It was ridiculous really and probably his own guilty conscience that stifled him, but still, he didn't truly breathe until he was well away from the house and discovery.

~*~

Daniel was happy to have escaped the insipient card play at Lady Crowther's soiree. It was the most wonderful thing when his daughter came to tell him that he was free to go find his amusement elsewhere. He knew he was quickly going to become indebted to the ladies of the Wagering Whist Society, but he didn't care. He was just happy when one of them offered to see Lydia home safely as had happened this evening.

"Good evening, my lord." Viscount Wickford greeted him soon after he'd entered the man's establishment. Powell's was quickly becoming one of the most popular places for a gentleman to seek solace and relaxation. Since it was a private club, Wickford was able to keep the membership exclusive.

"Good evening, Wickford. Any action at the tables tonight?" Lord Daniel asked.

"Lords Fetherington and Emmerton have had a difficult evening playing whist, each losing to the house a pleasing sum of money," Wickford said with a chuckle.

Daniel laughed. "Pleasing to *you*."

"Yes. I don't suppose Emmerton was very happy, but Fetherington doesn't much care. He's got enough that he can lose a few thousand and not even notice."

"I'm not sure I'm in the mood for whist," Daniel admitted, letting his eyes wander the club. They latched onto one man in particular—the one Lydia had gone out driving with the previous week. He'd hardly seen his daughter, they'd been so busy, and so hadn't had an opportunity to ask her if she ever found out the fellow's name. And he certainly wasn't going to admit to her that he'd placed himself in a strategic location within the park so as to be able to watch them as they drove by.

It wasn't so much as spying on his daughter, as ensuring for her safety, or so he'd told himself as he'd stood there watching each carriage as it had slowly passed him. He'd gotten a good eyeful of the gentleman she'd been with, but still was searching for a name to go with the face.

But now, it seemed as if luck was with him because the fellow was sitting just a few feet away. The man had a sizeable pile of coins sitting in front him as he peered at the cards on the table.

"What's happening there?" Daniel asked Wickford, nodding toward the table.

"Vingt-et-un. I'm sure they'd be happy for a fourth to join in," the proprietor offered.

"Who is that playing? I see Merrick and Touffington, but I don't know the third fellow."

"Ah, that's one of our newer members, Viscount Welles. Not a deep player, but he comes pretty regularly, so I can't complain. He's good friends with the Marquess of Cenway, so I couldn't easily deny him membership." Wickford gave a little laugh. "You don't want to alienate someone who will be a duke and in charge of a large fortune someday."

Daniel laughed. "No, I'm certain you wouldn't. Perhaps I will join them." You can learn a lot about a man from the way he gambles, Daniel thought, as he made his way over to the table.

Chapter Ten

"Good evening, gentlemen," Daniel said, taking a seat.

"Ah! Lord D—"

"Merrick," Daniel interrupted, giving the marquis a nod. "Is it too late to be dealt in?" He wasn't certain he wanted young Lord Welles to know who he was just yet. He always found that people opened up much more readily to strangers.

"No, of course not, my lord," the dealer said.

Daniel placed some coins on the table before taking a look at the cards that had just been handed to him. "All well, Merrick?" Daniel asked.

"Yes. How about with you?" his friend answered, keeping his eyes on his cards.

"Fine, fine. I was playing at Crowthers' soiree earlier, but more people were there to talk than play, I'm afraid," Daniel said.

"It was rather crowded," Lord Welles said, pushing a few coins into the center of the table.

"Were you there?"

"Yes. I try to attend a variety of parties. Makes my mother happy thinking that some lucky young woman might catch my eye," he said with a little laugh.

"And has any?" Daniel asked, also putting his coins in.

"There is one young woman who is rather vexing in her mystery," the fellow admitted. He then turned over his cards and declared, "Vingt-et-un, gentlemen."

Daniel gave a little laugh and a shake of his head. Merrick did the same, but Touffington scowled.

"That's the third time in half an hour, Welles!" Touffington complained.

Welles gave a little shrug. "I'm afraid I've had a particularly lucky evening, and it is persisting. Sorry, old man."

"With your mystery lady?" Daniel asked.

"Oh, no." Welles laughed. "Sadly, I haven't had any luck with her."

"What is it that confuses you about her?" Merrick asked. "Surely a woman couldn't be that curious."

Welles just laughed again and shook his head. "I haven't quite figured her out yet. She presented herself one way, and then, well, I'm not too sure if I was mistaken in my assessment of her." He took a glance at the cards just dealt to him and then looked up at the men. "I have a sneaking suspicion there might be more there than she's allowing me to see."

"Ah, but isn't that always the case with these females," Touffington said. "Always hiding things. Always sneaking that jab in just when and where you'd least expect it. God, I need a drink!"

"You've got one at your elbow," Daniel pointed out.

The man looked next to his arm, found his glass, and emptied it in a swallow. "Now I need another."

Daniel played another couple of hands, losing all he'd been able to afford to Lord Welles, whose luck was indeed holding. He then excused himself and decided to call it a night. He hadn't been able to learn the name of the vexing young woman the fellow had been talking about, but it couldn't have been his Lydia, could it? The question nagged at him all the way home.

~May 19~

Daniel couldn't help but replay his conversation with Welles the following night. Had he been referring to Lydia when he'd been talking about a young woman seeming to be more than he thought? Daniel didn't know, but he was definitely going to find out. It also wouldn't hurt the young man to know he needed to tread carefully in his pursuit of Lydia.

While it was true that Daniel wanted nothing more than for his daughter to get married, he also wanted her to be happy and marry well. She needed to marry the right man, not just anyone.

And so it was that Daniel found himself knocking on the door of the Welles home. What he hadn't expected was the handsome woman who answered the door.

She looked a little wan and tired, but her eyes sparkled with curiosity. They were the loveliest light blue. Lines on either side of them emphasized both her eyes and her age. It was clear she spent a great deal of time smiling. It took him a moment to recall why he was there.

"Good afternoon, madam," he said, giving her a slight nod. "Is this the home of the Viscount Welles?"

"Yes. May I help you?"

"Yes, I would like to speak with him if he is at home?"

She took a step back to allow him into the house and then admitted, "I'm afraid I don't know if he is or not. It's the oddest thing, but my staff seems to have disappeared."

He stopped just inside the door. "I didn't think a woman as beautiful and well-dressed as you could be the housekeeper," he admitted and then immediately wanted to slap his hand over his mouth. Where had that come from, and how could he possibly have allowed his inner thoughts to cross his tongue? He was a lawyer for God's sake. He never misspoke!

She just chuckled and flushed prettily like a young girl. "Oh, no. I'm not the housekeeper, I'm Lady Welles. But it is the strangest thing that no one is around." She turned and looked toward the baize door that must have led down to the kitchens. It remained stubbornly closed.

Daniel's reflex to protect jumped to the fore. "My lady, you do realize that you've just let a strange man into your house without even asking his name or for a visiting card? Why, I could be here to rob you."

Her beautiful eyes widened. "My goodness, you are right. Not only that, but I just let you know that I seem to be entirely alone here. My God, what an idiot I am!" She put a hand to her cheek and shook her head, giving him the most pathetic look. It just made him want to take her into his arms and promise to keep her safe from harm.

He couldn't believe his reaction. He hadn't felt this protective of anyone, aside from his daughter, for too many years. Not since Mary, his wife, died.

"...do you?" she was asking, but he completely missed what she'd said in his own shock at his behavior.

"I beg your pardon? Oh, a visiting card!" He guessed that's what she had asked for. "Yes, of course." He pulled one out of his pocket and handed it to her.

She squinted at it and held it away from her face. She read it silently and looked up at him. "A lawyer? Are you here on business, then, with my son? Is he expecting you?"

"Er, no. I did not arrange a meeting, but I did want to have a word with him if he's available," Daniel admitted.

She gave a nod. "Then you'll have to be patient as I go check to see if he's here. Why don't you come into the drawing room while I do so?"

"Shouldn't you perhaps first see where your staff is?" Daniel asked.

She gave a little shrug and then said with a little smile and a twinkle in her eye, "To tell you honestly, I've seen enough of them in the past month to last me a lifetime. I'm kind of enjoying this feeling of being alone in the house."

She gave a little laugh and led the way into a formal drawing room.

"I would hate to send you running upstairs just so I could have a word with Lord Welles," Daniel said, noticing how slowly she walked, as if that simple act was tiring.

"Oh, well, I could probably use the exercise."

"I beg your pardon, but you're already looking as if you've had quite a bit today."

She turned and gave him a sweet smile. "You are observant, aren't you, Lord Daniel?" She gave a nod and sat down on a chair, indicating he should do the same. "I'm afraid I'm still recovering from a terrible bout of influenza. In fact, if John knew that I was not only up out of bed but dressed and have left my room, well…"

"He wouldn't be pleased, I take it?" Daniel asked with a little chuckle.

"No! That boy has kept such a close eye on me for the past month… Well, it is because he loves me, I know that. And it has been just a few years since he lost his father—also to influenza—so you can't blame him for being a little over-protective."

"I am sorry to hear that," Daniel said.

She gave a little nod. "We go on now, don't we?" She paused and then looked appraisingly at Daniel. "When did you lose your wife?"

He nearly jumped back. "How did you know I lost her or that I was married at all?"

She gave a little laugh. "You are well dressed but clearly without a woman's eye—your coat and waistcoat don't quite match. They're similar but not quite right."

"I would think that would be the fault of my valet," he commented, looking down at his clothing.

"Men, even valets, don't always notice these things, but women do," she said. "And secondly, you were horrified to learn there was no one here but me. Your first instinct was that of protection, so clearly you are a man who is used to caring for a woman. And also, a man as handsome as you would never get away without marrying. So clearly, you must have been married but are no longer."

Daniel could only laugh at her astute observations. "Well, I am impressed. Yes, I was married, but my wife died many years ago—thirteen to be exact. And I am used to caring for a woman, but she is my daughter."

"Ah, so you haven't remarried?"

"No," he said, turning away for a moment as memories assailed him. "Lydia… Well, my daughter has needed my attention and all the love I could give after her mother died. I'm very sad to say the girl was in the room at the time and rather traumatized by the event." He turned back to Lady Welles. "Childbirth," he explained.

"I am sorry!"

He gave a nod of acknowledgement. "Both Mary and the baby—a boy—died."

"How awful for you and Lydia. It sounds like you were both hurt by it."

He gave a nod. "It hasn't been easy, but Lydia is a good girl. She's always been a happy child, always laughing, always smiling."

"Have you ever thought there might be something more behind her smile? People process grief in a lot of different ways," Lady Welles said, her voice softening.

Daniel stopped to think about it. "I don't know. I suppose I never even thought her laughter might be hiding anything." He paused. "I suppose I was just happy that she was smiling—that she *seemed* happy."

"Perhaps you were too busy to think anything more it? Or were too busy with your own grief," she offered.

"Yes, yes, I suppose I was." How could it have never occurred to him that she might be hiding her sadness and the pain of losing her mother behind a façade of happiness and giggles?

And last night Welles had said the young woman he was interested in was hiding something from him, he'd been sure of it. Now Daniel was absolutely certain that young woman was Lydia—of course!

"You've just thought of something," Lady Welles said.

Daniel started. "What? Oh, yes." He laughed. It had clearly been much too long since he'd been with such a clever, observant woman—not that Lydia wasn't clever, she probably was just so used to him that she didn't point out when he gave his thoughts away. "I met Lord Welles last night at my club. He was talking about a young woman he'd met and, well, I have to admit I came today to discover if that young woman was my Lydia and if so—"

"Learn more about him and his interest in your daughter," Lady Welles said, jumping in and completing his sentence.

Daniel laughed. "Yes, precisely. But something you just said made me think—makes me certain—that it was, indeed, Lydia who he was referring to. So would you mind, from a purely dispassionate view, naturally, telling me about your son?"

Lady Welles burst out laughing. "Dispassionate observation of my own son, of course!" She chuckled quietly to herself for another moment before saying, "John is a good boy. Well, a good man, I suppose I should say. He's become quiet since his father died—although he used to be quite the outgoing sort before that—so you might not realize it at first, but he's quite intelligent. He likes reading history and takes some interest in the running of his estate. It's not a large or particularly profitable estate. I should tell you, we're not well-off, but he's not hunting for a girl with a wealthy father either."

"Well, that's good, because as you saw, I work for my living. Third son of a marquess," he added quickly to explain why he'd been reduced to such circumstances but still remained a member of society.

"Ah," she nodded her understanding. "Younger sons always have the more difficult route."

"Yes, and it really is too much to expect both of my older brothers to pre-decease me without heirs. And I have to admit that I rather like my nephew from my oldest brother. Very nice fellow. I wouldn't want anything to happen to him either."

She gave a laugh. "It's such a shame when that happens, isn't it? So, here you are, reduced to earning your living."

"Yes. Although, I quite like the law. But here I am doing exactly what your son would rightfully become furious with me over."

She shook her head, not knowing what he was talking about.

"I'm keeping you from your bed. You see, you are not the only one who is observant here. You're looking exhausted."

She put a hand to her cheek. "Oh, dear, am I?"

"Yes." He stood and came to help Lady Welles to her feet. She leaned on him a great deal confirming what he'd suspected.

When she was on her feet, she looked up at him. "Will you come again, Lord Daniel? I have so enjoyed our conversation."

"As have I, my lady. And I would be honored to call upon you again."

"Excellent. I'll send 'round a note when John is here so you can meet him as well."

"Actually, I would rather meet with you again instead, if you don't mind."

"Ah, well, in that case, I'll send a note when he *isn't* here." She giggled.

He gave a little laugh and then stepped back to bow to her. "I would like that, thank you."

Chapter Eleven

~May 21~

Lydia watched with fascination as the ladies of the Whist Society discussed the fate of Tina Ayres and the Duke of Warwick, but she just didn't have the heart to join in today. Normally, she loved participating in a friend's romantic interests. Not that she was an expert matchmaker, but she had been known to pair up a few friends.

Tina seemed to be very much in love with the Duke of Warwick, but he'd had the misfortune to propose on the very night she had been introduced to society as Lord Ayres' daughter. Before that, she'd merely been known as an up-and-coming modiste. It was all very romantic how Tina had come to London to try to better herself with the help of her mother, Lady Norman. Sadly because Tina had been born on the wrong side of the blanket, her mother couldn't claim Tina as her own for fear of destroying both their reputations. But then Tina's father, Lord Ayres, learned of her existence and decided to not only claim her as his own but introduce her to society and endow her with a very handsome dowry, making her very desirable to a number of gentlemen in search of a wife.

It was at this auspicious time that the duke decided to declare himself, making Tina think he'd only done so because of her new status. Clearly, the duke was truly in love with the girl, but he hadn't been aware that she'd been presented. How awkward it was for everyone involved!

Lydia thought that perhaps she should be just a little bit jealous of Tina who now had two serious suitors—the duke and Lord Ainsby, who had been actively pursuing her ever since the duke's disastrous proposal. Somehow, Lydia just couldn't muster up the feeling. No, she thought sadly, she simply didn't want to marry.

Yes, she'd promised her father she would try her best to become engaged by the end of the season, but she honestly had no intention of marrying anyone, ever, for with marriage came children and with children came death. She'd watched her own mother die attempting to give birth to a baby boy. Both had died that day and with them her father's heart and Lydia's desire to have children of her own. She'd only been seven at the time, but that was certainly old enough to understand and make a choice that would determine the rest of her life—which she hoped would be a very long one.

So what she really needed, she realized with a start as she watched the ladies plot how to help Tina marry the man she loved, was a man to propose to her. If she became engaged, Lydia thought, then her father wouldn't worry about her, and he would stop putting pressure on her to marry. She could enjoy the season and, once it was over and Lydia had fulfilled her promise, she could call off the engagement and return to her happy life taking care of her father and teaching the children of the miners in Doncaster.

But who could she convince to enter into a sham engagement with her? She wasn't that close to any gentleman to whom she could reveal that their engagement would be a sham, and she certainly wouldn't give false hope to someone who truly wanted to marry her. That would be too cruel.

If only she knew a gentleman... Oh. Oh, yes. Oh, my goodness, yes!

Lydia knew exactly who could and would enter into a fake engagement. For a moment she had to work hard to contain her giggles.

~May 22~

"Thank you so much for meeting with me again," Lydia said as she allowed Lord Welles to help her up into his phaeton.

"Of course." He gave the reins a snap and then said as he pulled forward, "I appreciate the discretion you've shown over the past week."

"I realize you have very little confidence in my abilities, and let me just be clear that I have very little regard for you, but I believe we may be able to come to an understanding," she said.

He raised his eyebrows and shot her a surprised glanced. "You get straight to the point, don't you?"

"I see no reason to draw things out."

"Nor engage in social niceties, I see," he said mildly.

"No. What I am proposing is more along the lines of a business deal, and the closer we keep it to such an arrangement, the easier it will be."

"You have me intrigued," he admitted as he negotiated his way into the stream of traffic making its way around the park.

She waited until he had finished making the complicated maneuver and then continued, "In exchange for my silence regarding a certain behavior of yours, I need you to agree to stop doing what it is you are doing—"

"Let me stop you right there, Miss Sheffield," he said, interrupting her. "I have absolutely no intention of ceasing my, er, operations. I've got people who depend on me and I will not let them down."

"I understand that, my lord, but there has *got* to be another way," Lydia persisted.

"Do you, perhaps, have a great deal of money which you could donate? That is the only way I could possibly agree to stop."

Lydia frowned. "No. Naturally, I do not. My father works for what money we have, as so many of the people you help do."

He turned toward her. "He *works*?"

"Yes. Do you not know who my father is?"

"No. I have to admit, I haven't made inquiries," he said, turning back toward the traffic.

"My father is Lord Daniel Sheffield, third son of the Marquess of Ashburnham, and a lawyer," she told him with a lift of her chin.

"A lawyer," he repeated as if to himself.

"Yes. So you can be sure that should I decide to tell anyone of your activities, I *will* be heard by those who have the providence to do something and put a stop to you for good." She didn't like threatening people, but she felt in this instance that it was warranted.

Lord Welles kept quiet.

"We will continue our discussion another time of how we might replace the income that would be lost if I stop my operation," he said after a minute. "What was your other condition?"

"I would like you to propose to me."

Chapter Twelve

Lord Welles pulled up the reins so hard, his horse let him know in no uncertain terms that she was not happy. The carriage also came to a quick halt, causing all sorts of problems for the one behind them.

"I say!" the man called out from the back.

"Sorry!" Lord Welles called back. He loosened the reins and they continued on. "What would you like me to propose, Miss Sheffield?"

"Just what you would expect, my lord, marriage."

"I'm sorry, but did you not say when you joined me this afternoon that you didn't particularly like me?" he asked, looking at her curiously.

"It's not that I don't like you, necessarily," Lydia started. She quickly stopped herself, however, not wanting to get into that cesspool of confusion. "But that's neither here nor there. I want you to propose to me so my father stops nagging me about getting married."

"Oh, I see." He visibly relaxed.

"Yes. I assure you, it won't be a real engagement. At the end of the season, I'll call it off and then we can continue on with our lives as we wish."

"And you will assure me that you will do just that," he confirmed.

"Yes, absolutely!"

"And for that you will not tell your father—or anyone else—that I, er, help myself to diamonds owned by other people."

"Exactly. If I tell anyone about your hobby—which I absolutely wouldn't—then you may reveal to the world that our engagement is a sham." She then added, "It would destroy my reputation as well."

He thought about that for a minute and then slowly began to nod his head.

"All you need to do is pay marked attention to me for a week or so—a dance or two at a few parties, another drive through the park, and then it will be completely believable to anyone that we have come to an understanding."

"I see."

"You *do* dance, my lord?" Lydia asked.

"Of course."

"Good."

"Just to make it believable that we would become engaged?" he clarified.

"Yes. My father wants me to marry for love, but he'll understand if I wish to marry someone I feel I could get along with and then learn to love later," she said, turning her face away. She didn't know why, but her chest suddenly felt tight. She blinked to clear her eyes a few times before turning back to the business at hand. She *would* keep a level head about this, she absolutely would!

Lord Welles didn't say anything but just gave a nod.

"You might try smiling every so often," Lydia added, turning her own lips up as she said so. "I am known to be rather funny, and if you don't find me so, who is going to believe that we shall suit?"

He gave a little laugh—a true one, she thought.

"I actually do find you rather amusing in an odd way," he said. "I have yet to figure you out, but that is a discussion for another time, perhaps." He turned and looked at her rather appraisingly for a moment, one side of his lips quirked up into a smile. "Very well, Miss Sheffield, I *shall* propose to you."

"Excellent! Next week, perhaps?"

He turned back to face the front. "In my own time."

"But not too long from now—" she started, suddenly worried that he would keep promising to do so but never actually follow through.

"I assure you, you will know."

Lord Welles took advantage of the fact that traffic had come to a stand-still. He turned to her, cupped her cheek in his hand, and looked deeply into her eyes. She hadn't noticed the gold and green flecks in his brown eyes before, nor how long his dark eyelashes were. His cheeks held the slightest shadow of a beard, but with his high cheekbones and narrow face it looked rather dashing. "Miss Sheffield, I promise you won't be disappointed," he said, smiling at her.

It took Lydia two breaths or more to control the sudden pounding of her heart and to remember this was probably just part of the show he had promised to provide. Well, he certainly didn't waste any time getting started on fulfilling his promise, she thought. She managed to smile in return and gave a little nod. "Thank you," she whispered.

She cleared her throat. "And you could probably call me Lydia."

Lord Welles's attention was pulled forward as traffic began moving once again. "Thank you. It's a very pretty name. I'm afraid mine is rather boring. My given name is John."

"Oh, but that makes sense," she said, suddenly remembering something she'd heard. "You're the Jack of Diamonds, then."

He gave a laugh. "Yes, I am. You've heard of my little calling card."

"Yes, of course, I think everyone in society has."

"I don't use it very often, only when I take something from a jewelry box or a safe."

"But naturally you can't leave it when you remove a piece from a lady's person," Lydia said, thinking it through.

"No."

"But then, you must have a number of decks of cards all missing that one card," Lydia said with a little laugh. She didn't know why she found that amusing, but somehow it tickled her funny bone.

He burst out laughing as well. "Yes. It is rather awkward, I have to admit. I can't tell you how many decks of otherwise perfectly serviceable playing cards I've given away to the children of the Rookeries. They don't mind that there's one card missing."

~*~

John joined his mother in her room that evening for dinner. She had been doing remarkably better, but he still insisted she keep to her room for the most part. She had admitted to leaving it for a short time the other day and said she'd enjoyed it a great deal, but more than that, she wouldn't say.

It was odd because he couldn't imagine what she would have done that she wouldn't wish to tell him.

He had quizzed the staff, but no one had even seen her leave her room. John wondered if it had simply been a dream she'd had while resting.

"I have some news," he started after they'd been served their dinner by the fireplace in her room.

She looked up at him expectantly. Was her color high? Was she feverish? No, she hadn't had a fever for over two weeks.

"I went out driving with that young lady again this afternoon," he told her, deciding that perhaps he just wasn't used to seeing her looking better. Perhaps she was finally on the mend—he could only hope!

"Oh? Did she finally decide what she wanted from you in return for her silence?"

"Yes. She wants me to propose to her."

His mother choked and ended up coughing into her napkin. He jumped up to thump her on her back, but she raised her hand to stay him.

"It's all right. You just caught me off guard," she managed to say before coughing a little more.

"Of course." He sat back down and then waited until she caught her breath before continuing. "It wouldn't be a real engagement, naturally. She said she would call it off at the end of the season. It is simply to stop her father from putting pressure on her to find a husband."

"You know, you never told me her name," his mother said.

"Lydia Sheffield," he said before taking a large bite from his fork.

His mother's eyes went wide for a moment and then a smile split her face. "Oh, John, I am so happy for you!"

"Do you know the Sheffields?" he asked, his eyes narrowing.

"Oh, er, well, everyone knows the Sheffields. It is the family name of the Marquess of Ashburnham. Your Miss Sheffield must be his niece."

"Oh, yes, I suppose so. She said that her father was a lawyer."

"Yes, that's right. I mean, I heard that one of his younger brothers had gone into law. I don't know about the other. There were three brothers, but no girls in the family—at least as far as I know."

"You seem to be quite well informed," John said, wondering how his mother knew all this about Lydia's family.

She gave a little shrug. "Society is very small, John. Everyone knows just about everyone else. At one point, I had every eligible gentleman and their family memorized. That was before I met your father, naturally."

John shook his head in wonder. "But then you married Papa anyway."

"What do you mean, anyway? I held a great regard for your father! He was a sweet, handsome man. And not only that, he had such a strong moral code. He... He made me feel good about myself and the work I was doing with the children from the orphanage. I knew if I married him, the money I'd inherited would go to good use and not just be thrown away on fripperies or gambling." She paused to take a sip of her wine. "You wouldn't believe how many gentlemen said it was inappropriate for me to be working with the poor. But your father, he understood and fully supported it."

"I would expect nothing less from him," John said, remembering his father fondly. Never had there been anyone more devoted to helping the poor than his father. Sadly, it had nearly bankrupted him. John still had no way to rebuild or replace all that had been lost, although he was slowly working on doing what he could with the little he had. He had been taught well to give, but he refused to destroy even more of what they had left to support his charitable work—ergo, he helped others "donate" to his cause, despite their lack of consent.

"But this is wonderful, truly wonderful, John. You know I've been hoping you would find a nice girl and settle down," his mother said, putting her half-finished plate aside.

John couldn't help but laugh. "You wanted me to marry a girl for her wealth, but if Miss Sheffield's father is a lawyer, it's unlikely that they're wealthy. In any case, this isn't a real engagement. I just told you, she's going to cry off at the end of the season," he reminded her. For a moment, he wondered if the fever had somehow damaged his mother's mind.

"Of course, my dear, so you said."

Chapter Thirteen

Lydia was laughing at something Lord Ainsby had said when she spied Lord Welles—John—arrive. He was looking very well this evening. He was wearing his usual dark jacket but had on a slightly brighter waistcoat with silver embroidery.

She turned back to the gentlemen surrounding her. Lord Ainsby was telling a funny story that had Lord Rosebury, Mr. Hershawn, and Lord Rexford all chuckling. She smiled even though she wasn't really listening. No, she was admiring—admiring the fact that she was standing at a ball in London surrounded by four incredibly handsome, eligible gentlemen, and they were all doing their utmost to make a good impression on her. Not only that, but they were funny, handsome, and well dressed.

This, she thought contentedly, was happiness. This was living! She practically giggled simply with the joy of it. And yet, her mind kept going back to Lord Welles, John, who she'd just asked to propose to her so she could avoid becoming actually entangled with any one of these gentlemen of the ton.

These men all needed wives. They needed someone to run their households or host their dinner parties. And most importantly, they needed someone to bear their children.

Well, it wouldn't be her! Lydia was never going to have children. Ever.

She decided that on the day she watched her mother die in childbirth, and there was absolutely nothing anyone could say to make her change her mind. Lord Rosebury had already proposed to her, and she'd turned him down. She'd heard from some other gentlemen that Lord Rexford was thinking of offering for her, as was Lord Stenford. But she wasn't going to marry any of them, no matter how funny, rich, or well titled they were. No, she was going to have her sham engagement to John, and then break it off at the end of the season and happily go back to her ordinary life.

She looked around at the men talking and laughing. Would they abandon her once they learned she was engaged to marry someone else? She hoped not. They brought her joy, and there was nothing she wanted more in life than to be happy.

~May 24~

"Good evening, Miss Sheffield," John said, as he walked up to Lydia. She was, as always, surrounded by men. He didn't blame them. She was looking particularly beautiful in a white dress with deep green ribbons that brought out the beautiful color of her eyes.

She turned a bright, smiling face to him. "Good evening to you, my lord. You know Lord Rosebury, Mr. Hershawn, Lord Rexford, and Lord Ainsby?"

"Of course," he nodded to the men. He'd played cards with each of them at one time or another but didn't know any of them particularly well. They were social butterflies, and he avoided the men like that as much as he did the women.

"Lord Ainsby was just telling us the most droll story," Lydia laughed, turning back to the gentleman in question.

"Oh, I'm sorry to interrupt, but I was wondering if you wouldn't care to dance?" John asked. He'd promised to dance with her, and he was not one to renege on a promise.

The smile that lit up her lovely face was enough to make the awkwardness of interrupting her when she was flirting with other men entirely worth it. It didn't hurt that she was obviously choosing him over them, but he wasn't about to let that go to his head, not when he knew it was only because they had an agreement.

"Why, thank you, Lord Welles. I would love to dance." She turned back to the other men. "I do hope you will excuse me?"

"Of course." "Naturally," they all said at once.

John did feel good walking off with his prize, despite knowing he had no right to do so.

"You're doing well, my lord," Lydia said with a giggle after the first few turns had been executed.

"Thank you. It's been a while since I've danced, but I do believe I remember the steps," he said, giving her a smile.

She laughed. "That's not what I was referring to, but yes, your dancing is excellent as well."

"Oh, what is it that I've done well with, then?"

"You're dancing with me—and looking as if you're enjoying yourself!" she said with a laugh.

He chuckled. "Oddly enough, I am enjoying myself. It's been a while since I've danced, and I do believe I have the most beautiful partner on the floor."

"Oh, now you are doing it too brown, my lord," she said, as she turned away from him to carry out some steps with the lady to her right.

"I am doing nothing but saying the truth. I am having fun," he said when they'd come together once again.

Lydia laughed out loud but moved away as the dance prescribed.

"You know you can be quite charming when you want to be," she said, as they moved together once again.

He gave a nod of his head. "Why, thank you. As I say, it's been a while, but I think I remember how to do this."

"You've been charming before?" she asked with a giggle.

"Oh, yes, my friends and I used to come down to London every few months when I was at university. We'd go to parties we hadn't been invited to and flirt outrageously with every girl we found." He didn't mention that the first few times they'd done that John had had to be dragged along and had needed to learn how to be charming. But he'd learned well and happily it was all coming back him now.

Lydia laughed. "But, then, why did you stop?"

"I graduated and had other work I had to do," he said, giving her a meaningful look. "My, er, hobby."

"Ah, of course," she said, nodding.

The dance ended and he bowed to her. He was sorry the dance had ended just as their conversation had taken a more serious note.

"Would you care for some lemonade?" he asked, not wanting to release her back to her flock of admirers just yet.

"Yes, thank you. I am quite warm."

The refreshment room was slightly less crowded than the ballroom, John was pleased to find.

"You are now going to refrain from engaging in your hobby, isn't that right?" Lydia asked, as she watched an older woman pass by who not only had diamonds around her neck and wrists but in her ears and hair as well. John absolutely had to find out who she was and pay her home a little visit sometime soon.

"I don't recall agreeing to that," he admitted, turning back to Lydia.

She raised one eyebrow. "That was part of the agreement."

"No. It was something you asked me to do, but I neither agreed nor disagreed to it."

"Lord Welles," she said threateningly.

"Miss Sheffield, I told you, there are people relying on me. I cannot simply stop doing what I'm doing. People will go hungry," he said, lowering his voice.

She huffed out her breath, clearly not happy with this. "We will find another way of feeding them then, but you cannot continue with this! It is wrong in the extreme!"

"And lying to your father is not?" he asked, raising his eyebrow as well—two could play at that game.

"It is a different level of deceit altogether. No one is hurt or loses anything by my... And it's not even lying. We *will* become engaged," she said, defending herself.

"With the explicit intention of breaking it off as soon as the season is over. It is lying."

"It's not the same thing," she said, frowning at him. "Now promise me that you won't—"

"I say, I must object in the strongest manner possible," a man said, interrupting their conversation.

"I beg your pardon, sir?" John said, turning toward the intruder.

"Miss Sheffield, I don't believe I have ever seen you without a smile on your lovely face. Is this gentleman bothering you?" the man asked, looking John up and down.

"No! Oh, no, Lord Bolton, although it is very kind of you to ask. I'm afraid Lord Welles was just recounting the sad story of his favorite mare who was injured recently, and you know how such things distress me," she said, lying so quickly and convincingly John was a little shocked.

"Oh, that is awful!" the gentleman said, turning back to John. "My sincere condolences, sir!"

"No worries. I do apologize, Miss Sheffield, for distressing you so. I assure you, I, er, have the mare under the best care, and she will be right as rain soon enough. A few days rest and she'll be ready to ride."

"You'd best go easy on her at first, you know," the man said.

"I don't think Lord Welles would ever do otherwise, would you, my lord?" Lydia said, replacing the smile that usually graced her lips.

"I wouldn't dream of it! I always treat my animals as if they were a part of my household. Well, they are, aren't they?" he said with a laugh, trying to lighten the mood.

"Hah! My valet complains I treat my horse better than I do him! Know just what you mean," Lord Bolton said, laughing.

"Oh, no!" Lydia said, giggling. "You would never treat anyone badly, Lord Bolton. Why you are much too kind to do such a thing."

"You are too good, Miss Sheffield, too good, I say. Would you care to join the set that is forming?" the man asked.

"I would be honored. Lord Welles, don't do anything I wouldn't do," she said pointedly.

He gave a little laugh and nodded to her but promised nothing.

He might not steal any diamonds this evening, he thought, but that didn't mean he couldn't find out who the woman was who'd passed them earlier—just for future reference.

CHAPTER FOURTEEN

"No, I'm sorry, but I beg to differ, Lady Sorrell. Shakespeare *does* make good use of the chorus in his plays," Lydia argued. They'd somehow found each other in the crowded ballroom and, after the initial pleasantries, had fallen right back into the discussion they'd had at Lady Crowther's soiree earlier that week. "Just look at Romeo and Juliet, at Henry V."

"Yes, naturally in those plays, but he doesn't use the technique as prevalently as the Greeks did," Lady Sorrell said with a smile, keeping the debate friendly.

"Well, no," Lydia conceded. "It isn't an integral part—"

"But then why would he seek her out?" Lady Sorrell interrupted. "He knew she didn't dance, I think he was just trying to make her look bad—worse than a cut direct, I tell you," she said.

Lydia had no idea what her friend was saying until she felt a presence at her elbow.

"Oh, Lord Welles!" Lady Sorrell said, "How lovely to see you again this evening."

Lydia turned and looked up into her pretend suitor's eyes. He was staring at her oddly. "Is there something wrong, my lord?" she asked.

He immediately cleared the frown off his face. "No! Nothing at all." He gave her a smile and then turned it on Lady Sorrell. "Who was so rude, Lady Sorrell?"

"Oh, er… I'm sure you don't know him, my lord," Lady Sorrell floundered.

"Try me," he said, his smile growing harder as if he were daring her.

"You remember Miss Ayres. I introduced you to her the first time we went driving in the park," Lydia said.

He turned to her. "Oh, yes," he said hesitantly.

It was completely clear he had no recollection as to who she was talking about.

"We only stopped briefly to say hello," Lydia clarified.

His eyes opened briefly as he recalled the interaction. "Yes, I remember."

"She's a friend of ours," Lady Sorrell said. "And she's had such difficulties these past few weeks, poor thing."

"Yes. She came to London to be a modiste but has since learned that her father is Lord Ayres," Lydia said, picking up the story.

"He introduced her to society as his daughter, and she has been having the most difficult time of it, naturally, as so many ladies already knew her as a modiste," Lady Sorrell finished.

"Too many times has she had to deal with cuts and slights," Lydia said with a sad shake of her head.

"You might enjoy meeting her, my lord, she's very sweet," Lady Sorrell added. "She's just over there in the dress with the jonquil ribbons."

"Yellow ribbons," Lydia quickly clarified.

Lord Welles turned to her with one side of his mouth quirked up in a smile. "Thank you, Miss Sheffield. I wasn't entirely certain what color jonquil was."

She looked at him for a moment, trying to gauge whether he was serious or not. Finally, she giggled. "You're teasing me aren't you, my lord. You knew very well what color it was."

He laughed. "Yes, I'm sorry, but I did." He turned back toward Tina who was standing with her father, looking a little out of place. She was clearly trying hard to fit in to society, but still wasn't entirely there yet. "You know, I do believe I *will* go introduce myself. She looks decidedly awkward, and I've met Lord Ayres before. Perhaps she'll be kind enough to walk about with me." He gave Lydia and Lady Sorrell a little bow and then headed straight for Tina.

"She doesn't dance," Lydia said quickly before he walked away.

"So I understand from Lady Sorrell's sad tale," John said, before giving the ladies a slight bow and heading off in Tina's direction.

"Oh dear! I do hope he doesn't ask her about this supposed cut," Lydia said, watching him go.

"It would be exceedingly rude if he did, but it's all right because what I said actually did happen," Lady Sorrell said.

Lydia turned to her, her eyes widening. "No!"

"Oh, yes, I'm afraid so," Lady Sorrell said, still not turning her eyes from Tina.

Lord Welles had reached her, and they both watched as he bowed to her and her father clearly introducing himself. Tina and Lord Ayres both turned and looked over toward Lydia and Lady Sorrell.

Lydia raised a hand and waved, smiling.

Tina laughed and waved, before turning back to the gentleman in front of her. She gave him a curtsy and then tucked her hand into his elbow before allowing him to lead her away from her father. Lydia could see Tina giggling at something Lord Welles had said as they proceeded to promenade about the room.

Lydia had no idea why her throat suddenly became thick with emotion. It wasn't as if John was anything more to her than a means to an end. He wasn't a friend, barely an acquaintance. And yet, what he'd done was the most wonderful, kind thing she'd seen a man do in some time. Fiddlesticks! She didn't want to feel anything for him. She mustn't!

~*~

John bowed to Miss Ayres as she curtsied to him, and he returned her to her father's side. "Thank you, Miss Ayres, that was a most pleasant stroll about. I have to admit, I'm not particularly adept at dancing, but walking is something I can do."

"Now that is the most lovely lie anyone has told me this evening," Miss Ayres said with a laugh. "I saw you and Miss Sheffield dancing earlier and noticed how very graceful you were. However, I thank you for the sentiment."

"Really? Me? Graceful? Are you certain you don't have me confused with one of Miss Sheffield's other beau? She seems to have quite a few," he said, hating the feeling of jealousy that had suddenly come over him. How ridiculous! He had no right to feel anything when it came to Miss Sheffield. They had an agreement that was all—a matter of business, nothing more.

Miss Ayres giggled. "No, I'm quite certain it was you."

"Well, that is very kind of you to say." He gave a small bow suddenly feeling rather depleted. It was as if his well of charm had run dry.

It was odd, but after three years of perfecting being unnoticeable, suddenly having to not only make himself seen, but be amiable as well, was a bit more difficult than he'd anticipated. It helped that Lydia was such an outgoing person, he could leech some of her energy. Seeing how uncomfortable Miss Ayres had looked had somehow given him the internal strength to approach her.

It had been worth the effort, as well. She was a very sweet girl, and it seemed that everything Lydia and Lady Sorrell had said had been right. He'd quizzed Miss Ayres gently as they'd walked about the room—not about the supposed slight, naturally, but about everything else that they'd said. She'd been surprisingly forthcoming. She probably had no idea how to dissemble if she'd wanted to.

As he walked away, he couldn't help but notice the woman he'd seen earlier covered with diamonds. He'd learned that her name was Lady Wraxley, and according to the polite inquiries he'd made, she lived in a fortress with dozens of servants, closer to the river rather than in Mayfair.

He stopped just next to where she was standing and talking with some friends, other ladies about her age. As he watched her gesturing with her hands, her ring—a rather large affair with four nice-sized diamonds surrounded by a circle of smaller stones— slipped back and forth, up and down her finger. It was clearly too large. It would be such a shame if it happened to slip off her finger.

John immediately chastised himself. He'd told Lydia that he'd stop stealing and discuss with her alternative ways to support those who were relying on him, didn't he? He thought back to their conversation and then realized with some pleasure that he hadn't actually made any promises one way or another.

She'd told him to stop stealing and then they'd been interrupted. He'd not said whether he would or not.

The lady next to him finally lowered her hand to her side as her friend took over talking. Lady Wraxley nodded, thoroughly engaged in what her friend was saying. John took one step back and then started forward, "accidentally" bumping into the lady.

"Oh, I do beg your pardon, madam," he said quickly, pausing for only the merest second to slip her ring into his pocket. Was it very bad of him? He couldn't decide. He knew that this would feed at least five families for a month or clothe ten growing children for a year. No, he was doing the right thing, Lydia just didn't understand—how could she when she had never known a day's want in her life?

The fact that he simply couldn't stop himself from relieving a lady of her diamonds when they were practically being thrown at him was completely irrelevant.

Chapter Fifteen

"It was very kind of you to take Miss Ayres for a promenade the other night at the ball," Lydia said after John had made the difficult transition from the street to Rotten Row amongst the throng of equipages driving around the park.

He acknowledged her comment with a nod. "It wasn't difficult. She's a very nice young lady. I can see why you're friends with her."

Lydia gave him a bright smile. "She is sweet, isn't she?"

Strangely enough, the entire evening had been an excellent one for John. It was extremely unusual for him to feel so pleased with an evening as he had after he'd gone home to his bed after that ball. He'd done as he'd promised and paid court to Lydia, he'd spoken to some interesting people, and he'd even come away with a lovely diamond ring. There was only one thing that still nagged at him, though, and it was the same thing that had bothered him after the Crowther's soiree. He could see no other option but to simply ask Lydia straight out.

"Would you mind telling me what you and Lady Sorrell were discussing when I joined you— honestly?" he asked. He stole a glance at Lydia to catch her reaction to his query.

She raised her eyebrows and opened her eyes wide. "What do you mean? We were discussing Tina, just as we told you," she said.

"No, that's what Lady Sorrell quickly switched the topic to when she saw me approaching. Before that you were talking about something else entirely, and I'm afraid my curiosity has simply gotten the better of me. I'd like to know what it was."

Lydia turned and looked forward, staying silent.

"You did the same thing at Lady Crowther's soiree. It wasn't too difficult to tell either time, you know. At Lady Crowther's, it was you who suddenly changed the topic making Lady Sorrell quite confused. At the ball on Saturday, it was Lady Sorrell who did the same to you. Although, I have to admit you were much better at picking up the cues she was giving you and didn't look at all shocked at the sudden change in subject."

Lydia's mouth had dropped open just a touch, showing off her pink, full lips and a touch of her straight white teeth. A moment later, she was laughing behind her gloved hand, her beautiful green eyes twinkling with amusement. "Oh, John, you amaze me, you do!" she said when she finally regained control.

He smiled at her. "I'm so glad, but you aren't going to change the subject on me. I still want to know what you two were discussing so animatedly."

Her eyes widened. "Were we animated in our conversation?"

"You were indeed. What was the topic under discussion?" He paused and then added, "You can stop trying to distract me, and by the way, I'm simply going to keep asking until you actually answer the question."

She giggled again. "Very well, if you want to know the absolute truth."

"I do," he said, now nearly certain that's *not* what he was going to get.

"We were discussing the use of the chorus as used in ancient Greek theatre compared with the use of it in Shakespeare's plays," she said with a broad smile on her face.

John couldn't help laughing at that. What a faradiddle! What an absolute lie! She couldn't even come up with a plausible topic? "What do you take me for, Miss Sheffield, that you think I would believe that for even an instant?" he said, holding back further laughter. It was such a shame she didn't feel she could tell him the truth. He was truly beginning to like Miss Lydia Sheffield, but she was definitely hiding something from him.

She became rather serious, tilting her head a little as she looked at him. "And what makes you so certain that I'm not telling you the truth?"

"Well, first of all, I cannot imagine for one instant that you would engage in such an academic discussion. And secondly, that you would do so at a party."

"Well, that we should do it at a party is rather odd, I have to give you that. But, I assure you I am fully capable of having such a conversation. Lady Sorrell and I enjoy our little debates."

John stayed quiet or else he might call the young lady an outright liar to her face, which, he was certain, would be terribly rude. How could Lydia think he would believe such a beautiful, social girl—a diamond of the first water—would be both interested in and capable of holding such debates? Although, he did have to hand it to her in the creativity to even come up with such a topic. He wondered if she'd overheard some gentlemen having such a discussion—her father, perhaps? In any case, there was absolutely no chance that Lydia Sheffield would engage in such a conversation.

"Fine, Lydia, don't tell me what you were talking about. I'm certain I would find it as uninteresting as you would probably find an actual debate contrasting Shakespearean plays with that of the ancient Greeks," he said finally.

The girl turned her head away to watch the people walking down the side of the path they were driving on. He thought he'd caught a reflection of the light in her eye before she turned away from. It couldn't possibly be a tear, could it? Was she angry with him for seeing through her lie? Sad because... Well, he had no idea why she would be sad. No, it had to have been a trick of the light, that's all. She was interested in seeing who was out today so she could gossip about it with her friends later, that was all.

~May 25~

The back gate to the Welles' home was open, just as Lady Welles' note said it would be, when Daniel tried it that afternoon at three o'clock sharp.

He found the lady herself sitting underneath a small willow looking as delicate and beautiful as the drooping arms of the tree. He stopped and stared at her for a moment as he approached.

"You are right on time," she said with a little laugh. "But what are you doing just standing there? Come and join me here on this bench." She moved over a touch so that there'd be room for both of them.

"I was just enjoying the beauty before me," he said, sitting next to her.

"Oh!" She laughed and gave his arm a playful little touch. "You are a charmer, aren't you?"

He chuckled. "Now tell me how you are feeling today," he said.

"Even better than I was the other day when you visited."

"Excellent! Still on the mend, though?"

She gave a nod and a little sigh. "Yes, sadly, I am still not quite one hundred percent. But with your company, I'm certain to get there faster."

"I will do all I can to help you. If it means sneaking in to see you every afternoon, I will do so. By the way, why *did* I need to sneak in?" he asked, cocking his head in curiosity.

"Oh, because I haven't told anyone about you yet." She sat back with a happy smile on her face. "You are my little secret."

"Are you ashamed of me?" he asked, half-teasing.

"What?" She sat up. "No! Of course not."

"But you want to keep our meetings a secret," he pointed out.

"Yes. If I don't... Well, I don't know how John would react. He might think it was too soon after his father died, or he might be hurt that I was interested in meeting another man."

"I see." He took her hand, thrilled knowing that she was romantically interested in him. He felt the same way but had thought that maybe he was just being silly—that and the fact it had been so very long since he'd paid court to a lady. He was wondering if he'd just been overly hopeful that she'd enjoyed his company as much as he'd enjoyed hers. "Well, then, we'll keep this our little secret for a while longer."

"Thank you." She sat back again.

"You mentioned in your note that you had some interesting information for me as well," Daniel prompted.

"Oh, yes." She hesitated, clearly thinking about what she was going to say. She turned her gaze to her hands, playing with the fabric of her dress. "I... I don't know if I should tell you this. No, I'm almost certain that I should not, and yet... And yet, I feel compelled to do so." She looked up at him. "You should know."

He placed a hand over hers to still her fidgeting. "Whatever it is, it will be fine."

"But it's not my secret to tell," she said after glancing down at their hands.

He removed his. "Whose secret is it?"

She took in a deep breath. "Lydia's and John's, but I think mostly Lydia's."

He shook his head. What could Lady Welles possibly know of his daughter? "I don't understand. How could you know a secret of Lydia's?"

Chapter Sixteen

"Because, as I say, it is John's secret as well," Lady Welles said. "He confided in me—he tells me everything and always has. He's such a sweet boy! The only thing he's never told me about is his, er, liaisons, but I completely understand. I mean who would tell his mother—"

"Lady Welles," Daniel interrupted her.

"Oh, please call me Ann. We are friends now, are we not?"

He smiled at her. "Yes. We are good friends. But you were going to tell me something about my daughter, and I find that I'm rather curious as to what you were going to say. Please don't keep me in suspense any longer."

She giggled. "I'm so sorry. Of course!" She looked up at him, her sweet smile still lighting up her eyes. "You know that John has taken Lydia out driving a number of times and even danced with her at a ball the other night? He hasn't danced in ages!"

"I'm aware of the time they've spent together. Is this a secret? If so, it's an odd one as it was all done in public," Daniel said, confused.

"No, I'm getting to the secret part of it," she said. "Do you know *why* John's done all this? A boy who doesn't particularly like to dance and hasn't been out driving in the park since... Well, I think, ever!"

Daniel shook his head. "He's thinking of courting her?" It was the only reason why a gentleman would do such things.

Ann shook her head. "It's more than that."

Daniel wasn't sure what she was alluding to, but he said, "Dancing with Lydia would certainly allow him to fix her interest in him. She enjoys it a great deal. She enjoys anything that is light and fun and makes her laugh," Daniel said, giving Ann a smile.

"Like her father?" she asked.

"Oh, no. I'm a rather serious fellow," he said, forcing a frown onto his face.

She burst out laughing. "Oh, yes, of course, how silly of me to think otherwise."

"Indeed, my lady, you clearly don't know me well at all."

"But I look forward to getting to know you quite well," she said coyly.

That brought a true smile to his lips. But he still needed to learn more about what her son was up to and what this secret was. Ann had a very strange way of getting off the subject, but at this moment, he was happy to do so because he definitely wanted to know more about John, especially if he was interested in Lydia. "Is John a more serious sort?"

Lady Welles' smile slipped a little. "He is, but it's through no fault of his own. He was a very happy and carefree boy, but his father..." She paused, clearly remembering her husband. "His father felt it was vital that we help those in need. He taught that to John, of course."

"But that's a very good thing. I believe in it myself."

"Yes, I'm sure you do, but my husband took it to the extreme, I'm afraid."

"How so?"

She sighed, completely losing her smile. "He nearly bankrupted us, giving everything away. He pulled crops from the ground, paintings from the wall, sold the silver—everything he could to raise money to give to the poor."

"That is extreme!" Daniel agreed.

"Yes. There isn't very much left of the family's wealth. John has done what he could to repair some of the damage to the fields, at least. Everything else, well, it's simply gone and couldn't possibly be returned."

"So, John doesn't feel as his father did?"

"Oh, he does. He's simply not willing to destroy the family's legacy as his father was. He... He goes about helping the poor in other ways."

Daniel nodded. That was reassuring. So, if Lydia married Welles, she wouldn't be marrying wealth, but at least she'd be marrying a man who was balanced and doing his best for both his family and those in need. Truly, a father couldn't ask for more for his daughter.

"Apparently, Lydia has asked John to propose."

"What!" Daniel said, immediately pulled from his thoughts. "Why would she do that?"

Ann shrugged. "From what I understand, it is with the sole purpose of getting you to stop pestering her to marry. I understand that you've been rather persistent."

He gave a little nod. "I've given her this season to find a husband. A girl as pretty and intelligent as Lydia shouldn't have any problem doing so."

"Well, clearly she is unhappy with your ultimatum. That is the secret I've been hesitant to tell you. She has asked John to propose, and then at the end of the season, she says she'll break off the engagement. You see, she actually has no intention of marrying John—or perhaps anyone."

"John told you this?" Daniel asked, just to clarify she had her facts straight before he gave in to the burning fury that was beginning to simmer in his belly.

"Yes. They apparently went out for a drive last week. That's when she asked him to do this. He came home and told me about it, I suppose, because it was such a strange request."

"How did she know that he would be amendable to such a suggestion?" Daniel asked.

"I, er... I'm not sure."

"But why would she do this? I don't understand." Daniel got up and began to pace back and forth in front of Ann, trying to think this through and not give in to his anger. "She's a beautiful girl. She's already received two proposals of marriage from other gentlemen, who she turned down. And she is certain to get more." He stopped directly in front of her. "This makes no sense to me. They haven't even known each other very long."

"No, but perhaps they've connected in some way."

"Perhaps. Did John agree to this outlandish scheme, by the way?"

"Yes, apparently he did," she said with a sigh.

"I see. So she and John are planning on duping me—playing me for a fool—with a sham engagement just so that I stop pestering her to actually find a husband." He started pacing again. "It's not as if I'm forcing her to marry a man of my choosing! I'm giving her the opportunity to find love on her own."

He paused and turned toward Ann. "I had a very happy marriage with her mother. We were quite in love, which, as you know, is not common."

He resumed his pacing. "I just want the same thing for my daughter. Is that too much to ask? Is it wrong of me to want my daughter to be happy? But no, instead of doing as I asked and opening her mind and her heart, she's going behind my back, lying to me!"

"Daniel, Daniel! Stop!" Ann's voice permeated the anger growing stronger with each turn and thought.

He turned toward her again, pausing in his pacing.

She reached out and unclenched his fists. "Stop. You don't know what is going through the girl's mind. You don't know what's in her heart. I'm certain there's a very good explanation for what she's doing. You've said yourself that she's an intelligent girl."

He took a deep breath. "Yes. Yes, you're right. She is." He closed his eyes for a moment. "There's got to be a good reason why she's doing this." When he opened them again, he looked her in the eye. "And I'm going to find out what it is."

"No!" she said quickly. "No," she said again a little more calmly. "If you do that, she and John will learn I broke John's confidence and told you of their scheme. My son will never trust me again. Please, please don't confront her."

Daniel sat back down, keeping hold of Ann's hands. "I would never do anything to jeopardize your relationship with your son, but I must know why Lydia would do this."

"I understand that. Truly, I do. But there's got to be another way to find out. Does she... Does she have any close friends in whom she might have confided?"

Daniel thought about that. He knew she was close with Lady Sorrell. They got together and engaged in academic discussion every so often. There was Diana Hemshawe, another member of the Whist Society, who was the same age as Lydia. And, of course, there were the other ladies of the Ladies' Wagering Whist Society... "Wait. The Ladies Wagering Whist Society might know or would be able to find out."

Ann just shook her head, not knowing what he was referring to.

"It's a group of women, including Lydia, who get together every week to play whist. Instead of wagering for money—which some of them can't afford—they wager for secrets."

Ann's lovely eyes widened. "Secrets?" she whispered.

"Yes. Whoever has the fewest points at the end of a game must tell the other ladies her deepest secret. None of them shares that information—not with family members or friends. Lydia wouldn't even tell me if anyone has lost and had to tell a secret or not."

"What an unusual idea!"

"It is, I know, but it seems to work."

"They must have all become quite close as a result of this secret sharing," Ann pointed out.

"Yes, I believe so. Which means they may know why Lydia would do this, would enter into a fake engagement."

"Ah! I see! Excellent! That is where you must go. You must speak with these ladies."

He nodded. "I shall!"

"One thing," Ann continued. "From all you've told me of Lydia, I'm certain she would be a wonderful match for John. That is what made me divulge this to you in the first place."

"I have to admit, I had been thinking the same of John," he admitted.

"Well, then, we need to do something—and I have absolutely no idea what—to make this engagement real."

Daniel wanted to laugh. Now he was being asked to play matchmaker? "I couldn't imagine how." He paused, his mind already working on the problem. "Let me think about it. And maybe the ladies of the Wagering Whist Society can help with that too."

"Excellent. And we do have until the end of the season," she said with a little laugh.

"I suppose we'll have to meet and discuss this rather often, don't you think?" he asked, turning back to her with a smile. He liked the idea of having an excuse to come see Ann. He liked her. He liked her a great deal.

She reached out and took his hand. "I do think so. Most definitely."

Chapter Seventeen

~May 26~

"Sir, what an unexpected—but pleasant, very pleasant—surprise," Mr. Cartwright, the grocer said upon opening his door to John that evening.

"I apologize for not having come around for the past few weeks. I've been extremely busy, I'm afraid," John said, taking the man's proffered hand.

"Of course. I would expect nothing less. That you come as often as you do is greatly appreciated, I can assure you. Please come in, come in." The man led the way up the stairs and into their apartment.

It was almost as if John had never left. Mistress Cartwright was precisely where she had been the previous time he'd come and so was their little boy, playing on the floor. He did notice there were a few more candles about the room and that made him happy.

"Oh, sir, how lovely to see you again," the lady said with a little chuckle.

"Very nice to see you too, Mrs. Cartwright. And may I say how happy I am to see that your light has increased," John said, giving her a nod.

She laughed. "Yes. My husband has been so kind as to accede to your wishes and provide a few more candles for me to stitch by."

"Excellent. And for you," John said, squatting down on the floor.

"Do you have more tarts, sir?" the boy asked eagerly.

"No, not today, I'm afraid. I simply have this," John said, pulling a packet from his pocket and handing it to the child.

The boy looked at it and then up at John.

"Go on, take it," John said with a laugh.

The boy looked to his mother for permission.

She tsked and said, "It's like Christmas every time you visit, sir. What is it this time, Timmy?"

The boy hesitantly reached out for the packet, a huge grin on his face. "Thank you, sir."

"Well open it first. Perhaps it's something awful which you won't like at all," John said.

"Oh, no, sir, I'm certain that I would love anything *you* gave me," the boy said with all the earnestness of a child. He then opened the paper and ooohed as two small wooden horses tumbled out. He picked them up and examined them closely before jumping up and showing them to his parents.

"They are fine horses," his father said, ruffling his boy's hair.

"You do like horses, don't you, Timmy?" John asked.

"Ugh! Does he like horses! One need only pass him in the street, and he stops dead in his tracks," his mother said, laughing.

"Is that so?" John asked. "Well, then, I'm going to have you up on my Athena's back, now aren't I?"

"Athena, sir?" the boy asked, his eyes going wide.

"My horse. I didn't bring her with me this evening, but I promise to come by some afternoon and let you ride her."

"You're going to spoil the lad, sir," his father objected.

"Well, if he's got a way with animals as well as a love for them, I don't see why he shouldn't start learning more about them now. In a few years, when he's a little older, we can think of making him a stable-master's apprentice so he can learn how to handle them."

The boy's mouth dropped open. "*Cor*! You mean it?"

John laughed. "I do. But let's take things one step at a time. First, we'll see how you do with Athena, then you've got to eat well and grow a bit more to be strong enough to manage a horse, all right?"

The boy just nodded.

John stood up and turned toward the grocer. "Everything else is all right, Mr. Cartwright?"

"Oh, yes sir. Although..." He paused.

John waited. The man was his eyes and ears on the ground here in this neighborhood. If anything of interest was happening, he was the one who knew of it, which meant that John wanted to know of it.

"It's Mary Small, sir," the grocer started.

John frowned. He'd never actually met the woman, although he had heard her name a few times as one of those who struggled more than most. She had children, he believed, but he knew nothing of her husband. "What is it? Is she unwell or having more troubles than usual?"

"Well, sir, it's just that she's due to have another wee-one soon, but she hasn't been in to the grocery for a week or more. We're a little worried for her."

"She has children already, isn't that right?" John asked.

"Yes. She's got two. One is Timmy's age and the other a few years older. We haven't seen them either," Mr. Cartwright said.

"Her husband skipped out and hasn't been seen these past six months," Mrs. Cartwright added with a sad shake of her head.

"Could you possibly go over to her tomorrow, Mrs. Cartwright, to check on them?" John asked.

"Yes, of course, I'd be happy to." The woman nodded.

"Good." John fished a few coins from his pocket. "Here, take over some basics for them—eggs, bread, milk—just in case they're in need." He handed the money to Mr. Cartwright.

"Thank you, sir, we'll do that."

"And do let me know if there's anything further she needs just now. I always leave money at the Angel, as you well know, for emergencies. Don't hesitate to ask for it," he reminded the man.

He gave a nod. "Yes sir, of course."

John could hear his wife give a little tsk of her tongue. "The owner is a friend of mine," he reminded her, "and a good man."

"I know, sir, I know. I just don't like that it's a tavern we've got to go to for emergencies."

John gave a little laugh. "I understand. But it's one of the safest places I know."

He took his leave but stopped in to see Mr. Miller at the Angel to make sure he had the money John had left with him the last time. A brief word in his ear ensured that he was prepared to give as much as necessary to Mr. Cartwright should Mary Small need it. John trusted each one of his friends to do the right thing and to look after the woman and her children.

~May 26~

Daniel left for Lady Norman's home twice.

He'd sat in his study thinking through his conversation with Ann, but the only solution he could come up with was the one he'd mentioned to her—to speak to the ladies of the Wagering Whist Society.

It was probably the most awkward thing he could do, to speak to people he didn't know, about someone which he *should* know very well—his own daughter. He'd left his home with all the determination he could muster.

And then started to have second thoughts and returned to his study.

How was he even going to bring up the subject? How was he going to say, "By the way, would you mind very much asking my daughter something very close and personal, and potentially embarrassing and secret, and then tell me what she says?" One just didn't do that! And especially not to strangers.

But these ladies weren't strangers to Lydia. They were her close friends. The closest she'd probably ever had. And not only that, but ladies shared secrets with one another. They told each other how they felt and what was worrying them. Surely, Lydia had discussed with her friends why she didn't want to marry.

And so, he'd set out again, this time absolutely determined to go through with it, no matter how potentially embarrassing it was to admit to strangers that he didn't have as close a relationship with his daughter as he wished.

"Lady Norman, thank you so much for seeing me," Daniel said after bowing to the lady in question.

"Of course. You are Miss Sheffield's father, are you not?" Lady Norman asked, indicating he take a seat on the elegant gold-colored scrolled sofa.

"I am," he agreed.

"Well, then, I must thank you for allowing her to spend her Wednesday afternoons with the Ladies Wagering Whist Society. She is such a sweet young lady and a rather good whist player too," she said with a laugh.

"Thank you. I know that she truly enjoys being a part of your group."

"Now, what is it that brought you to me? I do hope that everything is all right with Miss Sheffield? I saw her not too long ago at a party, and she seemed to be in fine health."

"Oh, yes, she is, thank you. It's just... I have learned something disturbing, and I was wondering if you—and perhaps the other ladies of your society— might be able to help me."

Chapter Eighteen

Lady Norman widened her eyes and waited for Daniel to elaborate.

"It has been told to me, in the strictest confidence, that Lydia has asked a gentleman to propose to her in order to get me to stop pestering her to find a husband. She then intends on breaking this engagement at the end of the season."

"My goodness! Why would she do such a thing?"

"That is precisely what I am here to find out. Has she said anything to you about being against marriage? About being unhappy with the gentlemen she has met in London? Anything at all that you can think of that would make her decide to do this?"

"Goodness, gracious, no! Although, I have to say, she generally does not confide in me. I believe she and Lady Sorrell are closer, so you might ask her."

He nodded. "But she hasn't mentioned anything during the course of your card games?"

"Not at all."

"Do you think it might be possible to ask her? Or perhaps guide her to telling you if there's anything wrong?" He paused and shook his head. "I simply cannot understand why she would engage in this sort of subterfuge if there isn't a good reason."

"No, I agree. To ask a gentleman to propose with the intention of breaking the engagement... Well, that is quite serious indeed! Is the gentleman in question aware she plans on breaking the engagement?"

"Yes. He's fully aware of her plans."

"Then, perhaps, you could ask him?" Lady Norman suggested.

Daniel shook his head. "I'm afraid I can't. If he were to find out I knew of Lydia's plans, it would jeopardize the relationship between him and the person who told me of Lydia's plan."

"Oh. Yes, I see." Lady Norman turned and gazed off toward the window, clearly thinking. "She's never even mentioned her search for a husband, as far as I know. And certainly not any pressure she felt from you to find one. She is a very happy girl, always laughing about something or making light of something."

"That's the way I've always seen her too, but I can't help thinking there must be something deeper, something we cannot see that is disturbing her."

"There couldn't be a fear of marriage, could there?" Lady Norman asked discreetly.

"No! My wife and I had a very happy marriage. In fact, we were very much in love. It is what I've always wished for Lydia. I have made it clear to her my greatest hope is that she can find someone with whom she shares a great affection as her mother and I did."

"You were very lucky in that regard, my lord. Not everyone has such a marriage," she said quietly.

Daniel didn't know anything about Lady Norman's personal circumstances, and it wasn't his place to ask. Instead, he simply nodded. "Which is why this plan of hers confuses me."

"Indeed. The only thing I can suggest..."

"Yes?"

"Tomorrow at our weekly meeting we have a special event planned," the lady said, a little smile beginning to grow on her lips. "It is a secret known only to a few of us. I would appreciate it if you didn't share it with anyone, but the Duke of Warwick is going to be joining us tomorrow with the express purpose of proposing marriage to Miss Tina Ayres. The Duchess of Kendell, who is a member of our group and close to the duke, has arranged it."

"Is there a reason why this is happening during your weekly meeting?" Daniel asked, curious as to why there was going to be a marriage proposal at a meeting of the Ladies Wagering Whist Society.

"Miss Ayres is a particular friend of our little group, and the duke is a good friend of the duchess. He wanted a semi-private way to propose—private enough that the entire world wasn't witness to it, but public enough so that Miss Ayres would see just how much she means to him."

"I see," Daniel said, not entirely certain he actually did, but he'd go along with her explanation.

"Anyway, what I'm thinking is perhaps after Miss Sheffield witnesses the open display of affection such as I know the duke holds for Miss Ayres, perhaps she'll realize that she can have that too. Perhaps she'll reconsider her decision not to marry."

"Ah! I see." That did make some sense to Daniel. "That's not a bad idea."

Lady Norman gave him a smile.

"All right, then. Let's wait and see what she makes of this proposal by the duke to Miss Ayres. If it touches Lydia in the way we hope, then perhaps she'll call off this sham proposal."

"Yes."

"But if not?"

"Then we'll talk further, my lord."

~May 28~

All of the ladies of the Wagering Whist Society were immensely grateful to relax with a few hands of whist after Tina and her new fiancé, the Duke of Warwick, and their other guests had left.

"Oh my, what an afternoon," Lady Moreton said as they all took their places at the two card tables in Lady Norman's game room.

"Indeed!" Lady Blakemore agreed.

"I think it is wonderful of you to allow us our game despite all the excitement we've just had, Lady Norman," Diana Hemshawe said from the other table.

"Well, I certainly feel the need the for something ordinary just now. Although I am very excited and happy for Tina, an hour or so of calm will be very welcome," Lady Norman said.

The words had barely left her mouth when Mrs. Aldridge's dog, Duchess, suddenly decided to make her presence known. Lydia hadn't even realized the dog was there while the duke was proposing to Tina, and she'd kept absolutely quiet during the dust-up between him and Tina's foster-father that had nearly come to blows. But now that everything was quiet, Duchess seemed to just go wild.

The little spaniel suddenly started racing around the room in circles, her nails clattering on the wooden floor even as her little paws slipped on its slick surface. She found more purchase and speed on the carpet in the center of the room and raced around and around like a horse with a burr under its saddle.

"What is going on with that animal," the Duchess of Kendell protested. "Mrs. Aldridge, get that thing under control this instant!"

Mrs. Aldridge stood up, but she could only watch as her little dog ran wild this way and that. "What do you think I can do?" the lady protested.

"What's wrong with her?" Lady Sorrell asked, her eyes on the dog.

"I think she didn't get her afternoon exercise today. My footman who plays with her was unwell," Mrs. Aldridge said. "Duchess, Duchess, come to Mummy."

The dog suddenly shifted directions and came full speed at her owner, long ears flopping wildly as she ran. The woman, however, was so shocked she gave a startled scream and stepped behind her chair. "No! Duchess, no! Calm down! Oh goodness!"

The dog ran right around her and headed for the far side of the room, still at top speed, coming to a skidding halt just before she ran head-long into the wall.

Lady Norman walked quickly to the door, opened it just enough to stick her head out, and called for her footman. When the young man came in, she located the dog that had come galloping back into the center of the room. Duchess sat there as if everything was normal, and she hadn't just been going mad a second ago.

"Thomas, could you please take Duchess outside and play with her for some time?" Lady Norman asked the footman.

The young man looked at the Duchess of Kendell.

"No, not me, you idiot! The dog!" the woman practically screeched.

Lydia had the hardest time not bursting into laughter. Diana, who was sitting to her right, covered her mouth to hide her sniggering, but she quickly turned it into a cough.

"Yes, my lady, of course, I-I didn't mean to suggest she might have meant you, Your Grace. My-my sincere apologies," the footman stammered as his cheeks turned bright red. He scooped up the little dog and left the room quickly.

Diana fell into another fit of coughing, but Lady Sorrell wasn't nearly so polite and started to giggle, which in turn made Lydia start, and pretty soon everyone but the duchess was laughing.

"I do *not* see what is so funny!" the duchess protested. She then turned to the woman who was quickly becoming her nemesis. "This is all your fault! I think we need a rule—no animals allowed."

Mrs. Aldridge stopped laughing immediately. "What? No! I will not agree that. I always bring my little Duchess with me wherever I go. If she's not allowed..."

"Now, now, Mrs. Aldridge," Lady Norman began.

"If the Duchess of Kendell objects to my dog, *she* can leave the society," Mrs. Aldridge said, crossing her arms over her ample chest.

"What? *Me*? It is *your* dog! You will be the one to leave. Either the dog is banned or Mrs. Aldridge is," the duchess said, also crossing her arms.

"Ladies, ladies," Lady Blakemore said, standing. "Your Grace, it has never happened before that the dog has gone wild like this. She is normally very well behaved, but after all the excitement earlier and her lack of exercise, I think we can understand that—"

"I will understand nothing," the duchess said. "No animals!"

"Please, Your Grace, I think we've all had a tiring day. Think about it and do consider that we've never had trouble with the dog before now," Lady Norman said.

The duchess just glared at Mrs. Aldridge. In turn, that lady gave a little huff and sat back down.

"Now that is an excellent idea. Why don't we play cards? It will calm all of us down," Lady Norman said, also taking her place.

Slowly all of the other ladies took their seats, including the duchess who was the last one to do so.

CHAPTER NINETEEN

Silence reigned for the first hand that the ladies played. Even Lydia appreciated the quiet and found it peaceful after all the excitement. During the second hand, Lady Norman said casually, "I have to say I am rather relieved that Warwick has proposed to Tina and that's all squared away." She smiled at the duchess who was sitting across from her. "It is all thanks to you, Your Grace."

The woman lifted one side of her lips in what looked like a reluctant little smile and gave a nod of her head in acknowledgement. "I am very pleased Warwick is happy, and everything worked out well."

"I was a little worried Tina was going to begin to feel some pressure from her father to marry," Lady Norman continued. She then looked up from her cards at Lydia and Diana, to her left and right. "Have either of you felt pressure from your fathers to marry?"

Lydia shared a look of surprise with Diana. It was a rather direct question. But then again, Lady Norman was well known for being rather forthright.

"My father isn't overly concerned," Diana said with a shrug. "He's more interested in whether I win the races in which I ride."

Lady Norman gave a little chuckle and then turned to Lydia.

"The whole reason my father insisted on us coming down to London for the season was to find a husband for me," she admitted. She then gave the ladies at her table a little smile and added, "Although now that Lord Welles is paying such marked attention, he's not said a word."

"You must be very relieved, then," Lady Norman said, looking back down at her cards.

Lydia gave a little shrug. "My father hasn't been unpleasant about it, although he did give me a deadline."

"My son is still on the market, you know, Miss Sheffield," Mrs. Aldridge called from the other table.

The duchess frowned in her direction. "We are all very well aware of your son's marital state, Mrs. Aldridge. You've reminded us of it on more than one occasion."

The woman gave an offended sniff and mumbled, "I was just trying to be helpful."

"But you have no objection to getting married, do you, Miss Sheffield?" Lady Norman asked.

"What an odd question!" Mrs. Aldridge exclaimed. "Why would any young lady object to getting married?"

Lydia was grateful to be spared answering the question. She just smiled at Mrs. Aldridge and put down a card. "I believe it's your turn, Lady Norman," she said politely.

"Oh, yes, of course," the lady said, refocusing her attention on her cards. "Well, I'm sure your father would be very happy with whoever you marry," Lady Norman commented.

Lydia gave her a smile and returned her attention to her cards, happy that she wasn't going to have to deal with her father's constant questions about the gentlemen of her acquaintance for much longer. As soon as John proposed, her life would become much easier.

~*~

"Thank you so much for bringing me with you," Lydia said as she, Diana, and Lady Moreton pulled their horses to a halt in front of the Dorothy School for Boys and Girls. "Seeing Tina's foster-father and brother yesterday reminded me so sharply of the miners of Doncaster, where my father and I live, that I just felt horribly homesick! I am missing the children I teach—or, I suppose, taught—so very much."

"Not at all," Lady Moreton said. "We're always happy to have more help for the children, and they do so love our visits—well, especially Diana's," she said with a laugh as she descended gracefully from her horse.

Diana jumped unceremoniously from hers. "That's because I give them rides on my horse," she said, giving Lydia a bright smile.

"Do you really? I can imagine they would love that!" Lydia said.

"Well, some more so than others," Lady Moreton said.

"Yes, there are some who are frightened, but I'm working with them," Diana said.

"That is good of you." Lydia got off her horse and handed the reins off to a boy who would take hers and Lady Moreton's horse for a walk while they visited the children inside.

"And the fact you've had experience with children before will make things easy," Lady

Moreton asked as they started up the walkway to the front door.

"Oh, yes. They are so clever, the children I teach. They picked up on rudimentary addition and subtraction in no time. I'm sure I'll have no trouble at all here."

"That's wonderful!" Lady Moreton said, letting the knocker fall.

"It broadens their opportunities so they have the choice to go into mining like their fathers or do something else like work in a shop," Lydia agreed.

"Good afternoon, ladies," the matron said, greeting them at the door. "We've been expecting you."

A line of fidgeting children who couldn't have been more the four or five years old stood against the wall just inside the school's visitor's drawing room.

"This is our class of six-and seven-year-olds," the matron said, indicating the children.

"But they're—" Lydia stopped mid-sentence when all eyes turned to her. "Adorable!" she quickly finished, not saying what was truly on her mind. How could such small children be seven years old?

Malnourishment, she answered in her own mind. Of course.

The matron smiled at her. "They are good children," she continued with what she had been saying. "They have been chosen to receive your special attentions today."

"Each time we come, we get a different group. They rotate so as to give everyone the special treat," Lady Moreton explained quietly in Lydia's ear.

Lydia gave a small nod to show she understood.

"They will be split into three groups, seeing as there are three of you today." She turned toward

Diana. "I understand you will be taking the children one by one for a ride on your horse in the driveway?"

"Yes," Diana said, giving the children a smile. "And if I remember correctly... Was it Michael or Johnny who was too scared last time your group had a chance to ride with me?"

"It was Johnny!" they all screamed, bursting out laughing at the one poor boy. It was easy to see which one he was because he was a quiet one who looked to be on the verge of tears.

"Ah, yes, so he gets to go up first because he's going to be brave today, aren't you, Johnny?" Diana said with an encouraging smile.

The boy gave a silent little nod.

"Lady Moreton, shall you draw with the children again today?" the matron asked.

"Yes, Matron. I've brought materials for everyone. If we could use one of your classrooms that would be wonderful," Lady Moreton said.

"Of course. We'll have everything set up for you in the room just across the hall, if that should please your ladyship?" the matron asked.

"That would be perfect, thank you," Lady Moreton said.

"And what will you be doing with the children, Miss Sheffield?" the matron asked, turning to Lydia.

"Oh, I'd like to play some games with them if that's all right. I've brought some blocks and fruit. We're going to playing counting games. Who here knows how to count to fifty?" she asked the children.

A few hands shot up into the air but most just stared silently at her.

"I knows how to count to a hundred!" one little girl said proudly.

Lydia gasped. "Well then, you will be my special helper in teaching the others. Will you do that?"

The little girl smiled broadly and nodded before lifting her little nose into the air.

"Excellent!" the matron said approvingly. "Each group will spend time with one of the ladies for half an hour and then you'll switch, so everyone will get a chance to spend time with each lady."

After the first half hour had finished, Lydia realized she hadn't had so much fun since she'd left the little school where she taught. These wee ones were so quick, she nearly ran out of the cut up fruit she'd brought along for the children to add and subtract with—and, of course, eat. The hour and a half was nearly over when the sound of hysterical crying made her jump to her feet.

"What is that?" she asked the children. They just shrugged and went on with their game. It seemed as if it were something they were used to. Lydia, however, wasn't. She went out into the hall to investigate.

A young woman, heavy with child, was on her knees just inside the main door, clutching two children to her as she and the children cried together. The matron stood by waiting patiently.

"I beg your pardon, Matron, but is everything all right?" Lydia asked.

"Oh, yes. I'm terribly sorry for the disturbance, Miss Sheffield. This woman has to put her children into the school and is clearly having some difficulty leaving them. They'll be all right, though."

"Can she not afford to keep them?" Lydia asked quietly.

CHAPTER TWENTY

"No, and certainly not with another on the way. They'll be better off here, and Diana has already said she'll sponsor the two children for their first year here. If Mary still can't afford to keep them herself, we'll have to see if she'll be willing to do so again at that time."

Lydia's heart grew heavy with the thought of this family being torn apart because of lack of money, but at least the children would be well cared for at the school. "It is good of Diana, but still..."

"Yes." The matron stepped forward. "Now, now, Mary, you're going to make yourself sick if you continue carrying on like this. You know where the children will be, and you can come visit them any time, you know that," she said, gently pulling the children from Mary's grasp.

A maid appeared and ushered the children away. It then took both the matron and Lydia to help Mary to her feet.

"I'm so sorry, Matron," Mary sniffed. "I wish... I wish I could keep 'em."

"I know. But you need to concentrate on yourself and the wee one for now. And that husband of yours—"

"I worry that 'e's good 'n gone, Matron. I's not seen 'im for six months now," Mary said, sniffling. She wiped her nose on her arm.

"I am sorry to hear that," the matron said. "But don't you worry about your two boys now. We'll take good care of them."

"I knows it, Matron. Thank you."

While the Matron and Mary had been talking, Lydia had pulled the few coins she had in her reticule out and hid them in her hand. When Mary turned to leave, she reached out and slipped them to her. "Do take care, Mary," she said with a smile.

"Thank... Thank you, Miss," Mary said with a quick glance down at her hand. She slipped from the house and Lydia returned to the children.

~*~

"I must apologize again for leaving you so suddenly last night," Daniel said as they sat down at dinner that night.

"It's perfectly fine. I understand. Who was it who needed you?" Lydia asked.

"A gentleman whose father died. The moment the earl passed, his illegitimate son came and claimed all but the man's title. His younger, legitimate son called me in immediately to stop him from taking possession of the family house here in London. We're working with the steward to secure their estate as well."

"Oh my!" Lydia said. "Was this anyone I know?"

"Perhaps but I'm not at liberty to divulge their names. You understand."

"Oh, yes, of course. So who will inherit?" she asked, nodding to Michael to serve her some of the roast beef in the platter he was holding by her side.

"I've looked through the man's will, and it looks as if the illegitimate son has a strong claim, but we'll see." He allowed Michael to serve him as well and then said, "So tell me, how was your Society meeting yesterday?" Of course, what he really wanted to ask was whether seeing two people very much in love made her change her mind about her ridiculous scheme, but he couldn't do that.

"Oh, it was fascinating and so exciting! Tina's foster-father and brother showed up, and they nearly came to blows with the duke! It was a little terrifying."

"Really? Were they fighting over Miss Ayres?"

"Yes. Mr. Rowan, Tina's foster-father, said Tina was engaged to marry his son, but she argued that she had never agreed to that and, apparently, has been paying him handsomely to keep herself free from such an engagement. Can you imagine? He just wanted her to marry his son so he would continue getting money. I'm not entirely certain how that worked out, but the Duke of Warwick told him he would get nothing—neither any more payments nor Tina. Lord Ayres showed up as well and joined in the fray. It was all very exciting, I can tell you."

"It sounds it," Daniel agreed. "And did you learn anything from all this excitement?"

Lydia laughed. "Oh, Papa, you always ask that when I've experienced something new!"

"Well, I don't think it's an unreasonable question," he argued.

"No. I suppose not. And, yes, I did learn something."

Daniel smiled and leaned forward. Ah, here now, she was going to tell him she now understood that true love was indeed possible.

"I learned I'm rather homesick, actually."

Daniel nearly jumped back. That was the last thing he was expecting! "What's that?"

"Yes. See Mr. Rowan and his son reminded me so forcefully of the miners of Doncaster, which made me think about the children I teach there. I began to miss them terribly! I mean, I've been missing them, but I've allowed society to distract me."

"I see." This was not at all what he'd hoped would happen.

"Yes. But while we were discussing the events of the day afterward, I remembered Lady Moreton goes every so often to work with some children at an orphanage not far from here. I asked her if I might join her the next time she goes, and she told me that I could go today! Diana was going with her, and she was certain I would be most welcome as well. So, that's where I was all afternoon!"

"At an orphanage," Daniel repeated, frowning at his daughter.

"Yes," she giggled. "I had the most wonderful day! The children were so sweet, and we played number games just as I do with the children at home. I had such a wonderful day, Papa." She sighed happily.

Daniel's heart broke a little with that sigh. He was so proud of his daughter for working with the poor children, but he was also concerned about her future. How was she ever to marry if she wanted to do nothing more than teach mathematics to children? She couldn't survive on that. She needed a husband.

Perhaps Ann was right. Maybe he needed to concentrate his efforts on making her engagement to John a real one.

~**May 29**~

It was the people he'd met the previous night in the Rookeries, and the others who he knew were counting on him, that propelled John to knock on the door of the Sheffield home. It wasn't Lydia. No, her beauty and charm notwithstanding, he felt nothing for her—or so he kept telling himself.

"May I help you, sir?" the footman who'd just opened the door asked politely.

He could do this. Why was he feeling nervous? It wasn't as if this was an actual proposal. Goodness knows, he didn't want that, right?

"Good afternoon." He handed over his calling card saying, "Is Lord Daniel at home?"

The footman took his card, glanced at it, and ushered him into the house. "If you would wait here just one moment, please, my lord."

He disappeared toward the back of the house.

It was quiet, John noticed. He hadn't known exactly what to expect at the home of a young lady as social as Lydia. The sound of her practicing some musical instrument, perhaps? Or laughter as she entertained her friends? But there was none of that. Perhaps she wasn't home. Yes, that must be it. She must be out with—John didn't even want to think about who she might be out with.

"Oh, John! How lovely to see you!"

He was jolted out of his thoughts by the sight of Lydia coming from the hallway the footman had just disappeared down. She looked as beautiful as ever. Today she was in some sort of muslin dress with pretty little green and pink flowers all over it.

He bowed. "Good afternoon, Lydia. I didn't think you'd be home."

She cocked her head a little but then gave a little giggle. "I don't go out every afternoon. Michael just came to inform us that you were here."

"Ah. Yes, I've, er, come..."

"You are here to see my father?" she asked when he paused awkwardly.

"Yes," John admitted.

"Well, then, I'll let you get to it. Good luck!" she said, her smile turning hopeful and encouraging, or so John imagined.

The footman had returned as well and was standing just behind Lydia. He indicated John should follow him. As he did so, he heard Lydia's footsteps and she ascended the stairs behind him.

CHAPTER TWENTY-ONE

He was shown into Lord Daniel's study in the back of the house. It was a bright room, gathering the afternoon sun on a large mahogany table in the center of the room. Books of all sorts and sizes covered the table, along with a pile of paper and an ink stand.

It must all have to do with Lord Daniel's work, John thought before his attention was grabbed by the man himself, who was standing by a smaller desk set under the window. It too was covered in books and papers. John figured he'd better keep this short. Clearly, Lord Daniel was very busy. He probably had two different projects going at once.

"Good afternoon, my lord," John said, pausing to bow from just inside the door.

"Good afternoon. Come in, come in. Please do excuse the mess, we've been hard at work as you see," he said with a chuckle. He didn't mention who the "we" was, but perhaps he had a secretary working with him and had just stepped out.

Lord Daniel indicated John should take a seat in the small seating area between the two tables. "Would you care for a drink?" he asked.

"No, thank you, my lord." John wanted to keep his wits about him, and although a little Dutch courage might be welcome just now, he thought it best to abstain.

Lord Daniel gave a nod and took the matching chair across from him. "How can I help you, then?"

"I, er... I'm not certain if you were aware, my lord, that your daughter and I have enjoyed some time together of late," John started. He realized now, too late, he probably should have prepared for this.

"Yes, I have noticed." Lord Daniel propped his elbows up on the arms of the chair and interlaced his fingers. His eyes seemed to bore into John.

"Yes, well, I was wondering, my lord, if you would give me your permission to address her, er, your daughter, I mean. I'm- I'm not very wealthy, but..."

"You have an estate near Wales, do you not?" Lord Daniel said as John paused, feeling rather awkward about this whole thing.

"Yes, my lord."

"I hear that it's been stripped clean of anything of worth, but you've started rebuilding it," Lord Daniel said.

John sat forward in his chair. "Where did you hear this?"

His lordship waved a hand in the air. "I've been looking into your background should such an occasion occur," he said.

"You thought I might ask for your daughter's hand?" How could he possibly know he would do that? Did he look into every gentleman who showed an interest in Lydia—or just him?

"Well, as I say, I have noticed you paying particular attention to her recently. You've taken her out for a drive in the park three times in the past two weeks," Lord Daniel pointed out.

John caught his jaw before his mouth dropped open.

Lord Daniel gave John a look. "When you have a daughter, you'll understand."

Oh, yes, well, that did make sense, John supposed. He sat back again. "So, then, you know my situation."

"Indeed, I do."

"Well, then, may I have your permission?"

"If she agrees, when would you think of having the wedding?" Lord Daniel asked.

Now, that stopped John. He hadn't thought of that—especially since there wasn't actually going to be a wedding! "I, er, haven't thought that far in advance, my lord. I suppose it would depend on what Lydia wishes."

Her father nodded and gave him a little smile. John breathed again, feeling as if he'd just passed an important test. "Indeed. Ladies do tend to have rather strong opinions about these things." There was a twinkle in the man's eye that reminded him of Lydia.

"Yes, my lord."

"While we'll certainly discuss this in greater length, I would think a wedding held sooner rather than later would be preferable. Perhaps even before the season is over?"

John jumped forward again. "Oh, no, sir! Er, I mean, I doubt either Lydia or my mother would be able to arrange things that quickly. Er, doesn't Lydia need to arrange for a trousseau or something?" He cleared his throat. Somehow, his voice had become unnaturally high.

John could have sword he'd seen Lord Daniel's lips twitch with a smile, but it was gone before he could be absolutely certain. "Ah, yes, she might wish to do that. Although, I'm certain if she ordered the things now, they could be ready before the end of June."

"Perhaps we should ask her, sir." John swallowed. "And we may be jumping the gun entirely. I haven't even proposed to her yet. She might say no."

This time Lord Daniel did actually laugh. "She might. I would be extremely surprised if she did, but, yes, she might."

~May 30~

The following day John found himself once more on the doorstep of the Sheffield home. This time he actually was here to see Lydia.

The footman recalled him from the day before. "Good afternoon, my lord," he said, stepping back to allow John into the house. "Are you here to see Lord Daniel again?"

"Good afternoon... Michael, isn't it? No, I'm here to see Miss Sheffield if you please."

The footman beamed that John remembered his name. "Thank you, my lord. Yes, Miss Sheffield is at home to callers this afternoon. If you would just come this way, please. There are a number of gentlemen and ladies present."

This time Michael led him up the stairs to the drawing room on the first floor. Indeed, Lydia was sitting in the center of the room surrounded by people. She was clearly enjoying herself a great deal. She let out a laugh and began clapping. "Oh, no! Lord Ainsby, that is too much! You are a cad!" She laughed even harder and the gentleman in question clearly had no issue with being called such names. John figured it was in good fun.

"Oh! Lord Welles!" Lydia called out. "How wonderful! I am so sorry, you just missed the most amusing story from Lord Ainsby, but do come in." She stood up to welcome him with a curtsy.

Others stood as well. John recognized Lord Ainsby, Lord Rosebury, Mr. Hershawn, and Lady Sorrell, but the rest were unknown to him. Lydia introduced everyone, but the names were lost on him a moment after they left her lips.

He smiled and bowed to all and then took a seat next to Lady Sorrell. "It is a pleasure to see you here," he said. "I don't suppose you and Miss Sheffield were able to continue conversation on, what silly faradiddle did she come up with? Ah, yes, ancient Greek theatre?" He gave a laugh.

Lady Sorrell widened her eyes for a moment. "She told you we were discussing Greek theatre?"

"Yes, as if I would believe such a thing," he said with a smile that invited her to join in on the joke.

The woman stayed silent but turned away with a smile twitching on her lips. Clearly, she found the idea as amusing as he did.

"Lord Welles, how did you find the ball the other night?" Lydia asked, turning from Lord Ainsby to him.

"Why, excellent as always, Miss Sheffield," John answered.

"Did you enjoy your promenade with Miss Ayres?" Lydia asked, giving him a warm smile, which he felt all the way to his toes. How did she do that, he wondered? She made him feel special. As if he were the only man in the room she cared about. It was ridiculous, he was sure, but it touched him all the same. He quickly refocused his mind on the question she had actually asked.

"I did. She's a very nice young woman," he said, giving Lydia a warm smile.

"Did you hear she became engaged the other day?" Lord Ainsby asked.

"No, really?" John asked, turning to the gentleman. "She told me that she had been out driving with you a number of times and enjoyed herself a great deal, but I assume it is not you who I should wish happy?"

The man sighed heavily. "No, alas. But she is the sweetest of girls."

"Poor Lord Ainsby," Lydia said, patting his hand.

"It's all right, it's quite all right. I knew all along I was merely borrowing her for a short while. Warwick is a very lucky man," Lord Ainsby said. "And I believe, on that note, I shall say my adieus." He stood and so did a number of other people.

"It is getting late," Lydia said, looking at the clock on the mantle.

Lady Sorrell gave a little start when she looked at the time. "My goodness, it is much later than I thought. I need to get home and see to dinner—Sorrell asked me to invite some people over for an academic discussion." She looked directly at John and added, "It's going to be a very long and fascinating evening." Turning back to Lydia she said, "I'm so sorry you decided not to join us."

Lydia gave a laugh. "Oh, well, maybe another time?"

"Yes, absolutely. You and your father will have to come next time."

For a moment, John actually believed Lydia was serious about attending an evening of intellectual pursuit, but one look into her beautiful, sparkling eyes and he figured she was just being polite.

"Shall I see you tomorrow at Lady Wrexley's?" Lydia asked Lady Sorrell.

"Yes, absolutely. And we can, er, finish our discussion of Greek theatre," she said, giving Lydia a significant look.

Lydia just burst out laughing. "Yes, we really must. It's been going on for much too long."

With that, Lady Sorrell gave John a curtsy and left.

There were only Mr. Hershawn, Lord Rosebury, and a third gentleman whose name John couldn't remember.

"Shall we walk out together, Welles?" Mr. Hershawn asked, giving John a tight smile.

"Oh, no, thank you. I need to have a word with Miss Sheffield," he said, giving them a slight bow.

Chapter Twenty-Two

Mr. Hershawn didn't seem willing to accept that answer, however. He crossed his arms in front of his chest. "Well, then, we'll wait, won't we gentlemen?" he asked, turning to look at his two friends.

"That's quite all right," John said, wishing them gone already.

"Gentlemen, you are so kind, but truly I'll be fine. Lord Welles and I have something in particular we need to discuss," Lydia said, also trying her best to usher them out.

"What is it, then? Is it because he's a viscount and I'm not?" Hershawn asked, turning on Lydia.

"I beg your pardon?" she asked, keeping the smile on her face but clearly under some strain.

"You'll have a private word with him but not with me. I tried to have a private word with you last week and you shoved me out," Hershawn said.

"Come now, Hersh, perhaps it would be best if we left," Lord Rosebury said.

"No. No, I'm not going to leave. Not unless Welles comes with us. I'm not leaving him alone with her," Hershawn said, sitting deliberately on the sofa.

Lydia looked to John for help.

For a moment, he actually felt bad for Mr. Hershawn. He knew exactly how it felt to be the one shoved out or left out altogether. Too often, it had been him in that situation when he'd gone out with his friends. Then, he'd felt incredibly lucky to be allowed to go along at all, and if there were enough young ladies for each one of them, he got to be social with whoever his friends left for him. But it had happened on more than one occasion that there'd been three of them and only two young ladies, which meant that John ended up going home early all because he wasn't quite as outgoing as the others had been.

But today, strangely enough, the tables were turned. He was the one who was getting the most beautiful girl in the room. He was the winner and Hershawn had to accept that and go home. Only he wasn't and it was damned awkward.

A momentary impulse to gloat over his win was quickly squashed. Instead, he looked at Mr. Hershawn and said, "May we have a word for just a moment, Mr. Hershawn? I would greatly appreciate it."

The fellow was disconcerted by John's gentle tone. He got up and followed John to the further end of the room. "I apologize, I do most sincerely," John started. "But I've spoken with her father and received his permission to pay my addresses. I'm certain Miss Sheffield would much prefer to be alone with me when I do so. Now, I can't guarantee she'll say yes, but you've got to give a fellow a chance," he said quietly.

Hershawn took a step back and looked at John for a moment. He looked at him thoroughly, up and down, and then gave him a little smile. "Very well." He lifted his chin and added, "She won't, you know. She doesn't go for your sort. Quiet ones. She likes to laugh. She likes to have fun. And she likes gentlemen to be dressed at the height of fashion, not"—he indicated John's demure choice of clothing—"that."

John stood there and accepted the man's forthright appraisal because he knew so much more than this fellow did. "You're right," John said. "She does. And I may not be the man for her," he said in all honesty. "But that doesn't mean a fellow can't dream. But a dream will only ever be a dream if you don't do everything you can to make it come true."

Hershawn looked at him for a moment, sizing up John's words. He then gave a nod. "Very well. You're right. And Miss Sheffield is worth every bit of it of effort a fellow can give. Good luck to you." With that, he gave John a pat on his back and left with his friends.

John exhaled as he watched them leave.

~*~

"Whatever did you say to him?" Lydia asked, as John came back over to her. She had gotten rather nervous when Mr. Hershawn had become so stubborn about leaving. She knew he'd wanted to speak to her, perhaps even to propose, but she wasn't certain if he'd spoken to her father yet.

She knew John had, but still she was extremely impressed with the way John had handled the situation. He'd done so with grace and understanding—not that she'd heard knew what he'd said to Mr. Hershawn. For all she knew, he'd just threatened his life if he didn't back down, but the man had calmed down and left voluntarily, and for that she was grateful.

"Nothing of import. I asked him to give me a chance, that's all," John said with a little shrug and a smile.

Lydia couldn't help but laugh. "To give you a chance? But you don't need a chance. We already have an understanding."

"Yes, but Hershawn doesn't know that, now does he?" John said, his smile growing wider.

He was incredibly handsome when his face lit up that way, Lydia thought, almost taken off-guard by how attracted she was to him just now. It was almost a shame this engagement *wasn't* going to be real.

For some strange reason, Lydia's mind went back to the Duke of Warwick's proposal to Tina. It had been the most romantic thing she'd ever seen— until now. She remembered so vividly standing there watching the duke defending Tina from her foster-father and claiming her as his own. Once Mr. Rowan had finally backed down and left, the love shining from the duke's eyes as he got down on one knee and proposed had brought tears to Lydia's eyes. It was so clear he and Tina had something incredible—a true love—and both of them would do anything for the other.

To think of that and then stand here knowing John would never feel that way for her, nor probably she for him, nearly broke her heart. She would never have that. She would never know true love.

And yet, what John just did... It gave her a small taste of what it must feel like to be loved. Oh, she knew he was just doing this because he had to, because she was forcing him to do so. It was why he came to balls and danced with her. It was why he took her out driving and courted her publicly. It wasn't because he actually *wanted* to be with her. She knew that in the back of her mind. But she could still pretend, couldn't she? She could still imagine he'd done all those things because *he* wanted to.

She watched him now get down on one knee in front of her, where she'd seen a few men already. They'd thought themselves to be sincere in their affections—or so they'd told her. But even if she'd been willing to marry, she'd felt nothing for them. John, on the other hand, well, there *was* something. She didn't yet know what it was, but there was definitely something inside of her that he touched.

But it was nothing could she admit to it out loud and most definitely not here. Not now.

Lydia didn't even need to listen to his words, she knew what he was saying, and she knew them to be empty of any real intention. Never would he feel what the Duke of Warwick felt for Tina. Never would he desire her or protect her or look at her with such devotion and love. All this, it was the fulfillment of a bargain. It meant nothing to John but the knowledge that his reputation was safe.

She smiled at him and nodded when he presented her with a beautiful emerald ring but inside she wept.

Chapter Twenty-Three

That very evening, John accompanied Lydia and her father to Lady Wrexley's party. It was a little awkward with Lord Daniel in tow, but he was clearly intent on accompanying them. Lydia looked ravishing as always, but she truly came to life once they entered the party.

It was fascinating. She was like one of these new gas lamps John had seen in a scientific demonstration. You could light it and it was a lovely small flame, and then you could turn up the gas and it truly began to shine. Lydia was like that. The moment they entered Lady Wrexley's home, she truly began to glow.

"Good evening Lady Norman, Your Grace," Lydia said, approaching two older ladies John had seen but never been introduced to.

They turned, smiling at the three of them. "Good evening, Miss Sheffield. Lord Daniel, how lovely to see you again," one of the ladies said.

"May I present my fiancé, Lord Welles?" Lydia said, making room for John to enter their little circle.

"Your fiancé? Congratulations!" the first lady said, giving Lord Daniel a side glance before turning to John.

"Indeed, hearty congratulations, Miss Sheffield," the second lady said.

"Her Grace, the Duchess of Kendell and Lady Norman," Lydia said, indicating the second and then the first lady.

John bowed to the two women. "I am honored," John murmured.

"We are all members of the Lady's Wagering Whist Society," Lydia explained.

"I see," John said, giving them a smile. "What a fascinating group you must have. How many members are there?"

"We are eight—enough to make up two tables," Lady Norman explained.

"And we are most definitely an eclectic group," the duchess agreed.

"Indeed. I think it makes it more fun and interesting. But we mustn't discuss our Society when there is such exciting news as your engagement, Miss Sheffield," Lady Norman said. "And how apropos, considering our conversation on Wednesday."

Lydia just gave a little laugh and then held out her hand to show off the ring he'd given her. It had been one of the few pieces of jewelry his mother had managed to hide from his father when he'd begun selling off the family jewels to give money to the poor. John had been touched when she'd offered it to him to give to Lydia, especially considering she knew the engagement was only going to last the season. He would have to be sure to get it back when she called it off. It was rather a shame, though, the green emerald was perfect for Lydia with her vibrant green eyes.

The ladies oohed and aahed over her ring and then continued to do so as Lydia told them the tale of Mr. Hershawn's behavior and then John's proposal. As she talked, more people came over to join them, and soon there was quite a crowd surrounding her. John found himself unceremoniously pushed back and out of the way. Within minutes, Lydia was the life of the party. Even her father joined in, though he hadn't been present, naturally.

John saw no need for him to be there as his mind began to wonder what delights the Wrexley's safe held. He remembered vividly seeing the lady wearing diamonds on her wrist, around her throat, and in her hair at the ball where he'd met Miss Ayres. Their hostess didn't seem to be wearing many of her diamonds tonight, which meant they were somewhere in this house.

He slipped away to where he thought the study might be. A low fire burned in the grate in the room, just bright enough to see by and dispel the damp of the evening. Chairs and a sofa surrounded the fire, and a library table sat off to one side.

John did a quick examination of the room, including looking behind paintings in his search for the family's safe. It took him a few minutes, but he found it hidden behind a shelf of tall books. He'd just pulled his lock-picking pin from his pocket when Lydia's laughter rang in his ears. He started, looking toward the door, and then realized that it was just his imagination.

Still, he could see her so easily in his mind's eye, smiling and laughing...and then looking at him with a gentle, pleading expression as she asked him to stop stealing. She'd said she understood there were people relying on him. She'd said she understood there were people in need. But she'd also said there were others ways of helping them, and she would do everything she could to find those ways.

Strangely enough, he believed her. He didn't know how, but surely there had to be other ways besides his father's idea of selling off everything you owned and his own of selling off items previously owned by others. John didn't particularly like stealing from people, although the challenge of it was certainly entertaining. His guilty conscience afterward was never pleasant, but the joy of seeing little Timmy Cartwright's eyes light up when he was presented with a fruit tart was enough to keep John happy for days. And knowing women in need like Mary Small...

He set his pin into the lock and started working it.

But Lydia trusted him. She trusted he'd stop doing this, and something strange within him wanted to be deserving of that. He wanted to make her happy. He wanted to make her proud and to respect him.

No, there had to be another way to support the people who relied on him. He would speak with Lydia about it, and they would find a way. He put away his pin and replaced the books on the shelf.

He needed some air.

~*~

Lydia noticed the moment John slipped away. She'd been telling the tale of how he proposed, perhaps embellishing it just a touch to poor Mr. Hershawn's detriment, and watching as John got pushed farther and farther back. The man could have stayed by her side as her father had, but somehow he'd allowed himself to be shoved aside. It was true that people could be aggressive, but sometimes John just seemed too much of the opposite—too passive if that were possible.

The moment he disappeared altogether, Lydia felt as if the room had dimmed just a touch. The saddest part was thinking about where he'd gone and what he might be doing. Oh, she didn't worry for one moment he was off talking to other ladies. No, in fact, she was nearly certain he was doing nothing of the kind.

What she worried about was that he was searching through Lady Wrexley's jewels looking for diamonds. For all she knew, he had his hand in Lady Wrexley's safe even as Lydia stood listening to Lord Rosebury tease poor Mr. Hershawn. It had been a little funny and very awkward that the gentleman had insisted on staying at Lydia's home when everyone else had left. She was still grateful John had handled the situation so well, but then he had to spoil everything, to Lydia's mind, by disappearing in this way.

Just as she knew the moment he was gone, Lydia was keenly aware of when John reappeared. He managed to find his way to her side, which wasn't quite as difficult as it had been just a quarter of an hour earlier. Most people had moved off to share the news or seek out other amusements.

"Where were you?" Lydia asked, unable to keep a touch of bitterness from entering her voice.

He looked at her for a moment, perhaps trying to gauge whether she was angry or merely upset. "I went out for some air," he said finally.

"Truly?" she asked, not quite believing him.

"I would not lie to you. Would you care for a turn about the garden? It's quite lovely. There are lanterns and the air is quite refreshing."

She relaxed a little and smiled up at him. "Yes, thank you, I would love that."

She could see his shoulders come down a touch as well as he extended his arm for her to take.

Chapter Twenty-Four

He was right. There *were* lanterns and the garden was very pretty in moonlight. Lydia allowed her head to roll back on her neck. "Oh, it *is* nice!"

He gave a little chuckle. They walked in silence for a few moments, enjoying the fresh air and the growing quiet as they slowly moved away from the party.

"I would never lie to you, you know," he said quietly.

She turned to look at him. "I believe you. You're a good man, John."

"Thank you. It means a lot to me that you think so."

For a moment, she basked in her happiness, but her earlier thoughts intruded on her. "When I saw you disappear, I thought you had gone to help yourself to Lady Wrexley's diamonds."

"I admit I thought about it," he said. "But you said we would find another way to help the people of the Rookeries. Just as I asked you to trust me, I'm trusting you. I'm counting on you to find another way—and they're counting on you as well."

"Thank you for your trust and honesty. I wish I had an answer as to how we will continue to help them, but I don't just at the moment. I will find one just as quickly as I can, however. You have my word."

"Children will starve if we don't," he said ominously.

She couldn't bear the thought and let out a shuddering sigh. "This is a very unhappy topic for a couple who has just become newly engaged," she said, trying to lighten the mood.

"Would you like me to spout poetry at you? Liken your eyes to the new leaves of spring? The flush of your cheeks to a rose about to bloom? Tell you that your smile brightens my entire day and to hear you laugh makes my heart melt with joy?"

"But that's lovely! John Welles, you are a poet, or you have the sentimentality of one," she said with a giggle. Why was it when Lord Rosebury or some other gentlemen spouted such nonsense at her she could only laugh and think them ridiculous, but when John did it she felt something like flutterings in her stomach and her heart growing warm? How silly!

"No, I'm just widely read, that's all. I do enjoy reading the poets every so often, but they all write such nonsense," he said with a laugh.

"So those are not your words?" she asked. She had also read the poets but didn't recall seeing those exact words anywhere.

"No, they were mine but similar enough to what others have written," he admitted.

"But did you mean them?" she had to ask.

He paused in the walk and turned to her. His large hand cupped her cheek, and he looked deeply into her eyes. He was smiling. It was the smallest smile, just enough to show he hadn't become sad or so completely serious that he'd lost all sense of humor. "I did. You are without a doubt the most beautiful woman I've ever had the pleasure to know. You are funny and a joy to be with. You will only be mine for a short while, but I plan on enjoying every minute of it."

He leaned down toward her, and she knew he was going to kiss her. She probably should have stopped him. She probably should have stepped away. Instead she found herself rising up on her toes so her lips could meet his.

At first, it was just a featherlight touch of warmth and breath, but then it deepened and Lydia closed her eyes so she could do no more than feel and taste and experience everything that was John. But it was over much too soon, much before she'd had her fill of him.

"I'm sorry," he whispered. "I probably shouldn't have done that."

"I'm sorry you stopped," she admitted quietly.

He gave a little laugh before gently pressing his lips to hers again, but just for a moment, just a quick kiss.

"We should be getting back. You are certain to be missed."

For once, Lydia regretted her popularity. Still, she wondered whether he was telling the complete truth about not stealing anything. But at this moment, she simply didn't care.

~May 31~

Mr. Meir was sitting at their usual table when John arrived at The Angel the following evening. He stood and they shook hands, even as Mr. Meir made eye contact with the barmaid and ordered two tankards of ale.

"I hear congratulations are in order," he began as their drinks were delivered.

"Thank you. Was there an announcement in the paper? I have to admit, I forgot to put one in myself, but perhaps Lord Daniel did so," John said, startled that Mr. Meir knew about his personal life.

"No, or well, if there was an announcement I didn't see it. I have my ear to the ground, however, and it was all anyone in society was talking about—how the incomparable Miss Sheffield was snatched up by a quiet viscount nobody had ever heard of." Mr. Meir chuckled.

John smiled. "Yes, that just about sums it up."

"So how did you convince this beauty to marry you?" Mr. Meir asked, clearly just as curious as the rest of society.

John gave the standard answer he and Lydia had decided upon. "Love at first sight," he said with a little smile and a shrug. "There's just something about her which I could not imagine living without. Oddly enough, she felt the same way about me."

John had suggested they say it was a social alliance as he was in need of an heir and she loved children, but she had said no to that suggestion very quickly. She said no one who truly knew her would believe such a fabrication.

John wasn't so certain Mr. Meir was buying the instant love story either. "Well, however it happened, I'm happy for you. I just hope it won't alter our agreement," the man said with a lift of his eyebrows.

"I'm afraid it will," John said. This was the part he'd worried about all the way over. "Lydia knows about this and has specifically asked me to stop, er, relieving people of their diamonds."

Mr. Meir frowned. "And you're going to let a woman dictate what you do?"

John gave a little shrug. "She's right, actually. What I'm doing is wrong. If we want these people to donate to the livelihood of the residents of the Rookeries, we should ask not simply take."

"And people are just going to give their money out the goodness of their hearts?" Mr. Meir asked. He began to laugh. It started with a little chuckle, but within a moment, he was throwing his head back with a full, hearty laughter as if this was the funniest thing he'd ever heard in his life.

John managed a little smile and waited for his companion to stop. When he finally did, he became quite serious. "There are people relying on you, Welles. Relying on you for their daily bread. You can't simply stop supporting them. You can't simply say this isn't right and cease all of your activities."

John sighed. "I am well aware, I assure you. And I'll figure something out. I just can't—"

"You can and you will because you have to. Now, what do you have for me today?"

John pulled out the small velvet sack into which he'd put his takings for the past few weeks. He'd found it in one of the safes he'd burgled and thought it would be convenient.

Mr. Meir nodded approvingly. "Nice. Very nice." He quickly slipped a packet of his own across the table in John's direction.

"Now, see, that wasn't so hard. I'm sure if you simply go on doing what you're doing, your lady love will never know the difference," Mr. Meir said with a hard smile.

She would. John knew she would. Lydia was a great deal more observant than he'd originally given her credit for. She would know exactly what he was doing and when, and he wouldn't be able to lie to her.

John had nothing he could say, so instead, he simply stood up, his business concluded. "I think this is goodbye, Mr. Meir. I wish you safe travels on your return journey to Amsterdam."

Before he could say anything, the owner of The Angel came up to them. "Good evening, sir," he said, nodding to Mr. Meir and then John.

"Good evening. How are you Mr. Miller?" John said.

"Well, sir, thank you. Very well. Same can't be said for Mary Small, however, I'm real sorry to say."

"Oh? I do hope it's not the baby?" John asked, concerned.

"No, sir, at least, not so far as I know. I heard she had to turn the older two over to the orphanage, though. Couldn't afford to feed 'em any longer, sir," the man said, shaking his head. "Right broken up, she is. I gave 'er what you'd left, but it weren't enough, not for more than a few days, least-aways. She said she's got to eat for the babe inside and then feedin' two more hungry mouths... An' she felt bad rackin' up the credit with the Cartwrights too. I told 'er you would cover it, but she just cried and cried and said she was goin' over to the orphanage. Guess she felt it was the best thing."

The story broke John's heart.

"Awful devoted to them, she was," Mr. Miller said. "Carefully worked out a way to be home for 'em and hold down a job while they slept. But with the new one on the way, she ain't been able to keep goin'. Had to quit her work, and now she's given up the children as well just so they can get three meals a day.

"Now what do you think?" Mr. Meir asked John. Of course, he knew John would never be able to leave the woman in need.

"Here's a little something for her," John said, counting out some money and handing it over to the tavern owner. "I'll do everything I can to make it possible for her to get her children back as soon as may be." He turned to Mr. Meir. "I'll think about it and be in contact. When are you leaving?"

"Not for another two weeks. I'll expect to hear from you before then."

John nodded and left. He didn't know what to do. Mary and so many others just like her were counting on him. Was Mr. Meir right to laugh at the idea that people wouldn't just give money to them? He had no idea. The words had just come out of his mouth at the time. Maybe Lydia had a different plan in mind. At least, he sincerely hoped she did.

Chapter Twenty-Five

~June 1~

Ann was sitting underneath the willow tree when Daniel entered the garden as he had before. "How do you look more beautiful every time I see you?" he asked, coming up to her.

She giggled. "It must be because I'm getting better. The color is returning to my cheeks, and I have more energy."

He took her hand as he sat down next to her. "I can't tell you how happy I am to hear that because we have serious matters to discuss."

Her eyes widened and her smile began to slip from her lips. "Oh?"

Daniel nodded. "I am happy to report that I believe your concerns were unfounded."

She tilted her head a little. "What concerns were those? I have so many, you know. But wait, before you do, I want to hear how things went at the party last night."

He gave a little laugh. "That is what I was about to tell you. Your concern that John and Lydia would need some help making their engagement real is completely unfounded."

"Oh? What happened?"

"Well, as soon as Lydia made it known that John had proposed, and she accepted, we were immediately surrounded by well-wishers. For nearly twenty minutes, Lydia had to repeat the story of how Mr. Hershawn had nearly ruined John's proposal by insisting on staying until John left Lydia's drawing room."

Ann giggled. "Oh, yes, John told me how he'd had to take the fellow aside and plead with him to leave."

"Yes, poor boy," Daniel agreed. "Once everyone at the party who wanted to hear the story directly from Lydia had done so, they all went off to spread the news. John was very thoughtful and took Lydia out into the garden for a breath of fresh air."

"Oh, really?"

"They were out there for quite some time," Daniel added.

"I do hope that Lydia's hair wasn't disturbed when they returned," she said with a giggle.

"Just a little," Daniel said, with a little laugh of his own.

"Oh, how wonderful!" And clapped her hands. "You know, I was thinking we really should throw them an engagement party."

"That's an excellent idea. Are you up for it?" Daniel asked with a touch of concern. He didn't want her to overdo it and have another set back to her recovery.

"I think so," Ann said. "I may rely on you to do a bit of the work if you don't mind..."

"Not at all. And I'm certain Lydia can be counted on to help as well."

She gave a nod. "We'll need her to write out the invitations. And she'll also know who they should go to. I'm certain you have a few people you'll need to invite, and John will as well, business associates or other friends?"

Daniel shrugged. "There might be one or two, but I generally don't like to mix my law practice with my personal life."

"That's fine. And John doesn't have very many friends, but we'll invite Sebastian, the Marquess of Cenway, who is one of his closest friends from university. I don't know if Mark and Louise will be able to come, that's my daughter and her husband. They've recently had their second child, who I'm going to have to go see soon, now that I'm getting better." She put her hand on Daniel's arm. "You should see their first, he is the spitting image of John when he was a baby. Oh, my goodness, what cheeks! And a little laugh that just invites you to join in. What a special child!"

Daniel smiled. "I am looking forward to being a grandfather."

"It is wonderful! Yes, so we'll invite them...and who else?"

"All of Lydia's Whist Society friends, I would imagine," Daniel said.

"Yes, yes indeed!" She clapped. "Oh, Daniel, this is going to be wonderful! I do so love a party!"

"And I love seeing you happy," he said. He couldn't believe it, but he was beginning to wonder if he wasn't just a little in love with this woman already. She made him feel so good. And now that Lydia was truly settled, nothing could be better.

Ann's eyes went wide as she clearly thought of something. "Daniel, we need to tell the children!"

He shook his head in confusion. "Tell them what?"

"About us!"

"Oh." Daniel thought about it for a moment, but it did make sense. They'd been keeping their relationship a secret, but now that they were all going to get together at this party, it would no doubt be obvious he and Ann were well acquainted. "The only problem I can see is I'd rather hoped to be able to have a... Well, a more significant announcement to make along those lines, but, well... I'm still not—"

"You're not certain you want to make such a commitment after only knowing me for such a short time?" she asked, cutting him off. Her beautiful eyes became slightly worried.

"No, I'm pretty certain I *am* ready to make a commitment," he said, smiling at her and running a few fingers down her soft cheek. "I just want to wait until I'm certain John and Lydia are truly set. Can I ask you to be a little more patient?"

She gave a little sigh then nodded. "Yes, of course. So then, we'll simply tell them that we know each other?"

"Well, it couldn't hurt to let them know we've been meeting, could it?"

Ann gave a little giggle. "John will so shocked. I've never kept anything from him before, certainly nothing this important."

"He won't be upset, will he?"

"I don't think so. But it doesn't much matter. I am a grown woman."

~June 4~

Lydia closed her eyes as her carriage approached Lady Norman's home. How was she going to do this? How was she going to face her friends and pretend to be happy for hours when all she wanted to do was to go back to bed?

She's hardly slept since the night of the party when she'd told everyone of her and John's engagement. How could she when all she could think about was that kiss!

He'd kissed her!

He'd made her feel something when she'd been trying so hard to push aside all the positive feelings she'd begun to have for him.

But then he'd been sweet and wonderful and kissed her, and now she was lost. Torn between wanting to run away and wanting to run into his arms and stay there forever. How could she have even thought of doing something like this to such a sweet and thoughtful man?

Oh, yes, he was stealing diamonds from members of the ton—and in all likelihood had done so even that evening—but they could afford it, and the money was going to help the poor. Surely, it wasn't that awful.

No, she reminded herself. It *was* wrong and he had to stop.

And she had to stop feeling anything for him.

Her carriage pulled up outside of Lady Norman's house. Lydia shoved aside all her hurt, worry and confusion, pasted a smile on her face, and stepped out onto the sidewalk.

Oddly enough, everyone was already assembled when Lydia was shown into Lady Norman's drawing room.

"My goodness, am I late?" she asked, looking around at everyone seated around the room.

"Oh no! Not at all," Lady Norman said, getting up. "Come in. We were just having a cup of tea. Would you care for some?"

That was exactly what she needed, Lydia thought gratefully. It would calm her down and steady her. "Oh, yes, thank you."

She was handed a cup, but with it Lady Norman said, "I'm terribly sorry, but I have bad news for you."

She looked over at the duchess who was sitting with her lips pinched together, looking rather perturbed. She next turned to Mrs. Aldridge, who was sitting with her sweet, little dog, Duchess, in her lap. She was doing her best to keep the dog's quivering nose from the empty cake plate in her hand, but she did manage to look up and give Lady Norman a supportive nod.

What was going on, Lydia wondered.

"We were tallying the points, and it seems that you have the fewest," Lady Norman said.

"Me?" Lydia started. "But surely that can't be right. I won one of the hands we played last week."

"True, but sadly, it wasn't enough," Lady Norman said, turning her face away.

"I'm afraid it's your turn to reveal a secret," Mrs. Aldridge said, as Lady Moreton removed the empty plate from her hand and put it on the table out of the dog's reach. "Oh, thank you."

"Perhaps there's something—" Mrs. Aldridge started but stopped abruptly.

"It's extremely annoying, we are aware," Lady Moreton said, "but we did all agree to abide by the rules. Lady Norman told us about Tina. Today, it's your turn."

Lydia took a long, bracing sip of her tea. Could she tell them the truth? Could she share exactly what led her to her present predicament? And, indeed, what that predicament was? How ridiculous to be falling in love with a man she was engaged to and have that be such a serious problem!

But maybe sharing her problem would make her feel better. Maybe they'd have some advice. "Very well," Lydia said, setting her empty teacup down. "Well, I'm sure you all know I've recently become engaged to marry Lord Welles."

"Yes, of course," Lady Norman said.

"Congratulations," Diana added.

She gave Diana a smile. They were the same age and had become friends over the past month or so that they'd known each other, so she certainly understood better than anyone how much easier an engagement made things. Sadly, Lydia's engagement didn't make anything easier, just the opposite in fact. "Thank you. It's not a real engagement, however. I've promised Lord Welles that I would call it off at the end of the season."

"But why?" Lady Blakemore asked. No one else said a word, they all just sat there watching her—as if they... No, they couldn't have known, that was out of the question!

"Because I don't want to marry," Lydia admitted.

"Has your father been pressuring you to become engaged?" Diana asked.

Lydia gave her best smile, which she was afraid wasn't all too convincing. "He has, but it's not that. I simply don't want to get married—ever."

"Did you parents have a difficult marriage?" Lady Moreton asked gently.

"No! They were very much in love," Lydia said.

"Then why don't you want to marry?" Lady Norman asked.

Lydia closed her eyes for a moment before saying, "I watched my mother die in childbirth. I am never going to go through that. And the only way to ensure I don't is to not get married."

"Oh, you poor child!" the duchess said with feeling.

"How awful," Mrs. Aldridge agreed.

"That must have been very difficult," Lady Blakemore said.

"It was," Lydia admitted. "So, you understand now. My father has insisted I become engaged this season. He wants me to marry, but... I can't. I just can't."

Chapter Twenty-Six

"Does Lord Welles know about this?" Lady Sorrell asked.

"He knows I'm going to call off our engagement, but not about the, the childbirth," Lydia admitted.

"And he was all right with that?" Lady Norman clarified.

"Yes. He's a very kind man. When I asked him to do this, he was very willing. Apparently, his mother has been pressuring him to become engaged as well. Even though we won't actually get married, he can at least tell her that he tried," Lydia explained. She certainly wasn't going to tell them the real reason why John agreed to such a scheme.

"But you two seemed very happy together the other night at the party," Diana said.

"Yes, we were," Lydia agreed. "I like Lord Welles a great deal, but... But I just can't go through with it. I can't risk becoming...dying," she finished on a whisper.

"But not all women die in childbirth," Diana said. "In fact, most do not."

"Exactly!" Lady Blakemore agreed. "Why, I've had four children of my own."

"I've had three, and no one was there with me when Tina was born but my maid," Lady Norman said. "I survived it just fine."

"Yes, I know," Lydia said. "Clearly, not all women die. But my mother did, and many, many others do as well."

"Well, then you'd better stop riding in carriages because people die in carriage accidents as well," Lady Moreton said. Lydia's heart constricted. They weren't taking her seriously!

"And don't ride a horse over any fences," Lady Sorrell said, picking up on what Lady Moreton was saying. "How many people die of a broken neck when they fall from a horse?"

Lydia couldn't believe her good friend was joining in this horrid argument. Why wasn't she supporting her?

"My goodness, there are so many ways to die," Mrs. Aldridge said. "I'm certain more people die from something else than from childbirth." She gave a little laugh, making Lydia feel like a knife was being plunged into her chest.

Lady Blakemore too began to laugh. "Honestly, Miss Sheffield, you cannot let this silly fear of yours ruin your whole life." The knife plunged deeper.

Lady Norman joined in. "No, no, Miss Sheffield, just let go of this ridiculous notion and marry Lord Welles." And deeper, causing Lydia to swallow hard at the lump forming in her throat. But she would not show them how they hurt her. Oh no, that would be too embarrassing, and she'd already had enough of that for one day. She managed to turn the corners of her lips up into something that passed for a smile. She nodded as if she agreed with their hurtful belittling of her fears.

"He's a very nice man. I'm sure he'll understand your fear and feel as we do, that while it is true it happens sometimes, you cannot live your life in fear of small possibilities," Lady Sorrell concluded.

So much for friends and understanding.

~*~

John was his usual silent self as they drove away from Lydia's home. She, herself, didn't feel very much like talking either. She was still smarting from the dismissal of her fear the day before at the Whist Society meeting.

"Lydia," John began as they approached the park, "I think we should talk about what happened the other night."

She looked at him. He was frowning and looking very serious.

"It, it meant a lot to me," he continued hesitantly. "It made me feel—"

"I think you should stop right there, my lord." Lydia didn't want to hear this. She didn't want John to feel anything. She didn't want to feel anything herself. She didn't want to do anything but run back to Doncaster and forget this entire season ever happened. "We had an agreement," she reminded him.

"And after our walk in the garden, you still feel inclined to—"

"I not only feel so inclined, I insist upon it," she said a little more harshly than she'd intended. Where was her happiness? Where was her joy and lightheartedness? Even if she hadn't felt it in her heart, at least she'd always been able to pretend. "I beg your pardon, John. I'm not quite myself today." She tried giving him a smile.

"You do seem a bit out of sorts. Is there something wrong?"

"No... Well, yes, but it's nothing I can talk about, I'm afraid. But please, let us say no more about changing our agreement. I am afraid I am quite insistent upon it." She paused and then put her hand on top of his. "I'm sorry if I led you to believe anything else. The kiss was special, but I will not be swayed, not for anything."

He carefully navigated their way into the park itself and then said, "May I ask why? Why you want to keep up this pretense? Your father was so happy we were engaged. He was as bright and animated as you at that party. In fact, I don't think I've ever seen him outside of the card room at a gathering, and yet there he was, proudly standing by your side as you told the story of our engagement again and again."

"I know, and I'm well aware he's going to be very unhappy when I break off our engagement, but it can't be helped." John was absolutely right in his assessment. Lydia had never seen her father so happy as he had been at that party. He was clearly thrilled with her engagement. She could only hope he would be understanding when she broke it off. He'd always supported her in what she wanted to do, and she prayed this would be no different.

"And if you felt anything when I kissed you..."

"You know I did!" She did her best to keep the smile on her face.

"Then, can you explain this to me? Why you are insisting on breaking our engagement?"

Lydia almost laughed. After her "friends" had belittled her fear, there was absolutely no possibility of her telling John the truth. Oh, no. She was going to keep this to herself from now on. "I'm sorry, but it's something... Something I can't share."

After a night of tossing and turning over her growing feelings for John and then her disastrous

Whist Society meeting, Lydia had come to the conclusion that she simply had to stop all this "feeling" nonsense entirely. She shouldn't worry about what her friends had thought of her fear, and she wouldn't feel anything for John. None of it was practical. None of it got her where she wanted to be, namely at home, living her life, teaching children, and not risking her life to bear some man's children.

He frowned. "Is there someone else?"

"What? No!"

"No one you'd rather marry? Someone you've already promised yourself to?" he persisted.

"I swear to you, there is no one—not here or at home."

He gave a short nod. "And there's nothing I can do or say that will change your mind?"

"I'm afraid not. Now, do let's turn to happier subjects. I can't have you looking so serious as we drive around the park. People will comment and think something is wrong between us."

John released the tension between his eyebrows but didn't look any happier, so she began to regale him with silly gossip. He didn't quite make it to laughing out loud at the antics of society, but at least he did quirk a smile.

~*~

John would have slammed the front door closed behind him if the footman hadn't been there to close it for him. He stomped back to his study, threw himself into the chair behind his desk and then threw himself out of it, and began to pace back and forth in front of the fireplace.

That wasn't satisfactory either. He needed to occupy himself. He needed to forget the feelings that Lydia had stirred inside of him. He needed to push aside the crazy idea he'd had that he might have been falling in love with her. He wasn't. He couldn't because she wasn't falling in love with him. She'd made that abundantly clear.

She was as determined as ever to hold to their original plan—their kiss, their laughter, the good times they'd had together be damned. It meant nothing to her. *He* meant nothing to her.

"John, is everything all right?" His mother stood in the doorway, wringing her hands and looking worried.

"Mother! What are you doing walking about? Shouldn't you still—"

"If you say I should still be abed, I will seriously consider taking that switch to you that your father refused to make use of," she said with no real malice to her words.

"I do beg your pardon. Please, be up, go visiting, take a walk in the park if you care to, but don't come crying to me when you fall ill once again," he snapped.

Now she truly did look hurt.

John sighed and went to her, stilling her hands with his own. "I'm sorry, Mother. I'm in a foul mood. Come in and sit down, please."

She did so but kept a hold of his hands, forcing him to sit with her. "What is it? What's happened?"

He shook his head, not certain he could share his frustration with her. It would probably make her upset. On the other hand, when had he ever kept anything from his mother?

"I didn't tell you, but at the party the other night, I... I kissed Lydia."

Chapter Twenty-Seven

A smile immediately brightened John's mother's face.

"No, don't become happy," he said quickly. "I thought it had meant something. She even admitted to me that she enjoyed it while we were out for a drive in the park. But she also told me, despite that, she's still as determined as ever to keep to our original plan. She refuses to even discuss the possibility of making our engagement real."

John just couldn't sit still and look at his mother's fallen expression. He got up and began pacing once again.

"I can't believe what an idiot I've been. Here I've been thinking perhaps I stood a chance with her. I thought just maybe..." He spun around toward his mother. "I gave up an opportunity to take an incredible diamond set because I knew she wouldn't approve! I told Mr. Meir that I was thinking of stopping stealing altogether."

His mother's eyes widened. "What did he say?"

"He told me I couldn't do that. He reminded me of all the people who are depending on me. It didn't help that Mr. Miller, the owner of The Angel, happened to come up to us just then and tell me that

Mary Small had to give her children to the orphanage because she can no longer afford to feed them."

"Oh dear, John, I'm so sorry."

He didn't know whether she was sorry to hear about Mary, or that he was thinking of not stealing any more. It didn't matter. "It's all right. I'm not going to stop now. It would be idiotic for me to do so when Lydia is simply going to break off our engagement and return to her home at the end of the season. I was thinking she would stay and help me raise money for the poor, but... Well..."

"She says she won't?"

"She says she'll be leaving as originally planned. So what is there for me to do?"

"And there is nothing you can do to change her mind?" his mother asked.

"No, apparently not." He dropped down into the chair across from her. "She is set on her course and will not even consider a change." He sat forward and added, "I even asked her why, but she refused to say."

His mother reached across the empty space between them and took his hands again. "We'll figure something out, John."

"No. There's no use. I just need to continue with this charade until the end of the season."

~June 5~

John was feeling rather particular this evening. After a few weeks of deliberately going back to the way he was at university—being more outgoing, dancing and trying to charm young women—it wasn't as easy as he'd thought it would be to disappear again. He'd enjoyed being social. It had been a fun diversion. But with Lydia making it perfectly clear their relationship would end with the season, he saw no reason to suspend his illegal activities and every reason to continue with them. There were people counting on him, and Lydia had made it perfectly clear she would not be there to help support them.

He slipped through Lady Clifdon's soiree completely unnoticed. His clothing was designed to elicit absolutely no attention, his expression was neutral, and he hardly made a sound as he moved through the crowded rooms searching for diamonds to filch.

At least he was certain he wouldn't see Lydia here tonight. This was definitely not her sort of affair. There was no dancing, no card playing, just discussions that leaned more toward the academic than the gossip and empty chatter so common at ordinary society events. But that didn't mean the ladies dressed any worse. No, he'd already relieved one lady of a small diamond bracelet and another of a few hairpins.

He slipped into the Clifdon's study to see if he could locate the safe but found the room occupied by a number of people making use of the extensive library, most likely to double-check facts that had come up in conversation. Yes, this was most definitely his sort of gathering.

He paused to listen to two men arguing about the exact route Alexander the Great took through Asia, and whether he truly did go as far south as India. John had read that he had, but the gentleman arguing against had some good points. But John wasn't here to actually engage in academic discussion. He needed to see if there weren't more pieces of jewelry he could relieve from their owners.

He was about to leave the room when he heard a familiar voice—but it couldn't be! He looked past the two men he'd just been listening to and simply could not believe his eyes!

Lydia!

Not only was it Lydia, but she was deep in conversation with Lord Pemberton-Howe, the celebrated anthropologist.

John was planning on attending his lordship's lecture the following week. The gentleman was in the country just for a short time to raise some money for his work before returning to his archaeological dig in Greece. But what was Lydia doing speaking with him? And what could they possibly be speaking about? Surely not who had danced with whom, that would be ridiculous. The gentleman wouldn't have any knowledge of who was who in society.

John edged closer in order to overhear their conversation.

"Yes, yes, you are quite right, Miss Sheffield," Lord Pemberton-Howe gave a little laugh. "It was, indeed, the muse Clio. My dearest wife made the connection nearly as quickly as you just did. What we haven't yet determined, however, was the use for these insets within the temple."

"Can you describe them to me? Are they the size of perhaps a missing statue?" Lydia asked.

"No, no, they're much larger than that. Five or six people could probably have stood in one comfortably," Lord Pemberton-Howe said.

Lydia frowned for a moment thinking about it, but then laughed. "You know what comes to my mind when you describe it like that is the chorus used in ancient Greek theatre. A friend and I were recently discussing their use."

Lord Pemberton-Howe smiled at her laugh, then clearly began to think about what she'd said. "My God! You're right! Could they have possibly had some sort of theatrical performance in the temple?"

"Or could they have taken the same concept of a chorus from the theatre? A chorus who explain the action, possibly some aspect of a religious service to onlookers?" she proposed.

Lord Pemberton-Howe frowned as he thought about it. "It's a very interesting theory! I will most definitely need to look into this further. What an idea! Fascinating, Miss Sheffield, absolutely fascinating!"

John couldn't believe it. Lydia. *His* Lydia was not only intelligently discussing archaeology with a renowned archaeologist but suggesting possibilities to him!

What happened to the featherbrained diamond of the first water he'd thought her to be—that she'd pretended to be? A fury like John hadn't ever felt nearly exploded out of him.

He stepped forward and gave Lord Pemberton-Howe a brief bow as he grabbed hold of Lydia's upper arm. "My lord, if you would be so kind as to excuse us. I need to have a word with Miss Sheffield. It's quite urgent, I assure you."

"John! What are you doing here? What? Where are we going?" Lydia protested as John started to drag her out of the room.

He didn't know where to take her as it seemed every room in the house was open to the public and occupied. He could think of nowhere else, so he pulled her up the stairs and into a bedchamber.

"John! I don't think we're supposed to be in here," she protested.

"I don't care just at the moment. It's the only private place I could think of," he snapped. "Now, just what the hell do you think you're doing?"

Lydia visibly recoiled from his strong language. "I beg your pardon?"

"You heard me. What are you doing here?"

"I think it's pretty obvious. I'm being attacked by my fiancé!" she snapped back. "What are *you* doing here, aside from being unnecessarily rude to me and Lord Pemberton-Howe?"

"I came... It doesn't matter why I came."

"You came to steal jewels, didn't you? My goodness, don't you *ever* stop? That was part of our agreement, you know. You were to propose to me and *stop stealing,* and I was not going to tell anyone of your nefarious activities."

"And I told you that I couldn't do that because I've got people relying on me. Besides, I did stop. When I told you at Lady Wrexley's ball that I hadn't stolen anything, I was telling the truth. I could have stolen her jewelry. I had opened the safe—but then I thought of you and I closed it again without taking anything."

"But then why are you stealing again?" Lydia asked, her eyes becoming worried.

"Because you're going to leave and I won't have any way of providing for the people who count on me," John told her. But then he remembered the real reason why he'd pulled her into this room. "You lied to me!" he said, pointing a finger at her.

Chapter Twenty-Eight

"What? When?" Lydia asked, completely confused. "I told you from the very beginning our engagement was going to end with the season. I never lied to you. It was you who wanted to change the terms of our agreement."

"Not that," he said dismissively. "You pretended to be a featherbrained socialite, and now I find you discussing archaeology with one of England's most famous archaeologists."

Lydia took a step back, her mouth dropping open a touch. And then she did the most unexpected thing John could have imagined. She started to laugh. She laughed as if he'd just said the funniest thing in the world.

"What's so amusing?" John asked. He was completely confused.

"You! You are absurd," she giggled. "*You're* the one who decided I was stupid. You started this whole thing on our very first drive. You told me that I couldn't possibly understand about the poor because I was beautiful—as if someone's looks have anything to do with how intelligent they are."

"But you... You encouraged my misconception," John said, thinking back to how confused Lady

Sorrell was when Lydia had suddenly changed the topic of conversation the moment John had approached them. And then another time when Lady Sorrell had done the same to Lydia at another party when John had joined them. He'd known Lydia was hiding something from him; he just hadn't been able to figure out what.

"Yes, I did because I was angry at your assumption."

"When I asked you what you and Lady Sorrell had really been talking about, you said that you'd been discussing the role of the chorus in tragedies," he remembered.

"That's right, and you didn't believe me," Lydia pointed out.

It was clear that John was the idiot now, and he didn't like it one bit. "You were telling me the truth."

Lydia just smiled at him and crossed her arms in front of her chest, looking so pleased with herself. "I think my work here is done." With a laugh, she turned and left the room.

John could only stand there, furious at himself and Lydia—but mostly himself.

~June 6~

"Diana, what a lovely surprise!" Lydia said as she joined Diana in her drawing room.

"I'm sorry to just drop in like this," Diana said, turning from the window where she'd been waiting.

"Oh no, don't be." Lydia said, indicating that they both sit. The maid came in with a tea tray, setting it on a side table. "Thank you, Sally, I'll pour," Lydia said, giving the girl a smile.

After being handed a cup of tea, Diana said, "I do hope you weren't offended by the ladies the other day."

Lydia widened her eyes, surprised that Diana had been aware of her hurt at the ladies' responses. A warmth of friendship rushed through her. How wonderful it was to have people like Diana in her life!

"I'm certain not one thing that they said was helpful—at least it wouldn't have been to me if I were afraid of childbirth," Diana continued.

Lydia blinked back the tears of gratitude that had suddenly sprung to her eyes and gave a little laugh. "No, I have to admit, it wasn't helpful at all. I'm certain they meant well... It's just..."

"Knowing they all survived the ordeal doesn't have any bearing on whether you will or won't. And besides, just telling you that they've had children doesn't alleviate your fear," Diana said.

Lydia couldn't help herself. She reached out and put her hand on Diana's arm. "Thank you. You understand. I can't *tell* you how much that means to me. I wish with all my heart I could just let go of this fear, but...but..." She gave a helpless giggle.

"Well, just hearing their stories isn't going to do it, I'm certain. I wish I knew what would," Diana said, placing her hand on top of her friend's.

"So do I," Lydia sighed. She pulled herself together again but wished she could support Diana as well. Of course, her father! Lydia suddenly remembered that Diana's father was horribly ill. "Please, tell me how your father is doing."

"Oh..." Diana's eyes saddened immediately, making Lydia feel awful for bringing it up. She'd wanted to help, not force her to think of something painful.

"Oh dear, was the doctor Lady Blakemore recommended not good or did he not come?" Lydia asked.

Oddly, Diana's cheeks flushed. "No, he did. He came today and he's wonderful!" Diana paused and took in a breath. "I mean, he seems very knowledgeable and intelligent. He told my father to drink some willow bark tea while he explores some other options for him, and he didn't once suggest cupping him."

Lydia looked at Diana sideways for a moment. So *that's* how it was. There had to be more to this doctor that Diana wasn't telling her. "I see. And tell me more of this Lord Colburne. Is he young? Old? Hunched with smelly breath?" She giggled.

Diana's cheeks turned a brighter pink. "He's not old—perhaps in his mid or late twenties. Certainly not hunched and I don't think his breath smelled."

"Well, that's good."

"Best of all, my father liked him and actually agreed to drink the tea."

"And you're looking forward to him coming back to visit again?" Lydia asked, so happy her dear friend had finally found a gentleman she found interesting.

"He said he would, and that he'd recommend further treatment. However, I have to apologize to you now. I know it's very short notice, but I don't think I will be able to make it to your engagement party tonight. I just wouldn't feel comfortable leaving my father alone for so long," she explained.

Lydia softened her teasing smile into one of understanding. "Of course. I don't blame you. I would feel the same way."

"Thank you. I feel bad, though. I would have liked to have met your father and Lord Welles's parents—I'm assuming they'll be there?"

"His father has passed, but Lady Welles will be here. I'll convey to them your regrets," Lydia said.

"Yes, please do. And to Lord Welles as well."

~*~

John and Lady Welles arrived a little before half-past seven that evening. Lydia had worked hard, conferring with the chef, making sure everything was exactly as it should be. She'd also handled all of the invitations, so she knew they were expecting twenty-three people that evening for dinner. Lady Welles had arranged the after-dinner entertainment, which Lydia knew consisted of musical performances by some of the ladies of the Whist Society as well as a well-known pair of opera singers.

"Good evening! Welcome, welcome," Lydia's father said a little too effusively when John and his mother entered the drawing room.

John bowed to her father and greeted him but quickly came over to Lydia. "You're looking very beautiful this evening," he said, a slight wariness in his eyes. He was probably wondering if she was still angry with him for assuming she was stupid.

She quickly put him at ease. "Don't worry, John, I'm not one to hold on to my anger, although I do always get even," she said with a sly smile.

He gave a relieved little laugh that held a touch of nervousness to it—as well he should be, she thought. "Well, I am happy to hear that. So we will have a pleasant evening tonight?"

"I expect so," Lydia said. She was about to tell him of the evening's program when her father interrupted.

"Lydia, Welles, Lady Welles and I have something we would like to share with you. Ah, but first, we all need drinks," Lydia's father said, clapping his hands together in anticipation.

He busied himself with pouring wine and seeing Lydia and Lady Welles seated comfortably. John sat next to his mother on the sofa.

"Thank you, Daniel," Lady Welles said after he handed her a glass. "Now, John, I don't want you to become upset, but Daniel and I have been meeting—just a few times—these past few weeks."

John turned toward his mother, his eyebrows drawn down. "What do you mean, you've been meeting?"

"I mean Daniel has been coming over to keep me company and chat," his mother said. "We have the most lovely garden, Miss Sheffield," she said, turning toward Lydia.

"Mother! I don't think Lydia wants to hear about our garden," John protested.

"No, I have to say, I'd much rather hear about your clandestine meetings with my father," Lydia said, turning toward Daniel and raising her eyebrows.

"They were hardly clandestine," he protested.

"Well, they were a little. I did tell the footman not to disturb me in the garden," Lady Welles admitted.

"But surely he did see Lord Daniel come into the house and escort him out to you?" John asked. "Why did he say nothing of this to me?"

"Because I didn't come in the front door," Daniel admitted a little sheepishly.

"What?" The word jumped from John's mouth.

"I left the back gate open for him, and he came in that way so no one would see him," Lady Welles admitted.

"But why?" Lydia asked.

Lady Welles shrugged. "Because it was more fun that way."

The sound of the knocker on the front door effectively put a halt to the conversation. "That must be one of our guests," Daniel said, looking toward the door.

"We'll continue this conversation later," John said, giving his mother a significant look.

"Oh, don't pucker up, dear. I am a grown woman and can see whomever I please. Now stand up and be polite," his mother said.

John clearly didn't like being treated like a child, but he did stand as the footman had just opened the door to admit the newcomers.

~*~

The party was going very well. Lydia was amazed because this was the very first dinner party she'd ever arranged. It was true, she had a great deal of help from Lady Welles, her staff, and the chef, but still, she was just thrilled with the way it was all going so smoothly.

And then, somehow, there seemed to be a lull in the conversation around the dinner table. It was as if everyone had just suddenly run out of things to say.

Lady Welles was seated at the foot of the table, Lydia's father at the head, and Lydia and John were seated in the center facing each other. When the room began to quiet, Lydia looked up from her plate. They were on the fish course—much, much too early for there to be a lack of conversation. She turned to Lady Welles for some sort of guidance. The lady, herself, looked rather startled.

"Do you know that Welles is doing the most amazing work in the Rookeries?" Lady Welles said, generally to the table at large.

It must have been the first thing to pop into her mind, and John clearly didn't approve. He frowned at his mother. "I don't think the assembled company wants to hear about that, Mother," he said.

"Oh, but we do!" Lady Moreton said from the end closer to Lydia's father. "What is it you do there? Do you work directly with the people who live there or go through the church, or some other organization, Lord Welles?"

John clearly had no choice but to answer her question politely. He pulled a smile onto his face and said, "I work directly with a group of people, and I donate to the church."

"How did you find people to work with?" Lord Blakemore asked.

"Actually, it was rather simple. I walked into a grocer's and asked if there were any outstanding debts owed to him by people in the neighborhood. Naturally, there were, so I paid them. I let him know that he should extend credit to anyone who needed and wanted it, and I would come by periodically and pay it off. I do the same thing with the proprietor of a secondhand clothing shop."

"But that's amazing!" Lady Moreton said.

John shrugged, clearly uncomfortable with the attention.

"Well, it's similar to what you did with the orphanage, my lady," Lydia said to Lady Moreton.

"Oh, well, but I went to a well-established organization," the lady said, turning slightly pink. "And I don't support them financially, I merely help with the children—I mean, I would donate if I could, but, well, circumstances..." she finished, her voice trailing off awkwardly.

"But what you do is just as important," Lady Norman said.

"It's true the children do enjoy our visits—Miss Hemshawe and Miss Sheffield have also come to work with the children," Lady Moreton said.

"You've gone as well?" John asked, looking across the table at Lydia.

"Of course. Going there reminds me of the children I used to teach in Doncaster," Lydia said.

Her father gave a little laugh. "You do miss them, don't you? She used to go just about every day and spend half the day there teaching the children of the miners."

"I do miss them terribly, but now I'm meeting the sweetest children at the orphanage, thanks to Lady Moreton. Although, to call the school an orphanage isn't exactly right, is it?" Lydia asked, looking at Lady Moreton.

"What do you mean?" the lady asked.

"Well, when I was there last week a woman came in and left her own two children. They aren't really orphans, but their mother, sadly, can't afford to feed them and knew they would be well cared for at the Dorothy School."

"Oh, that's unusual, I'm sure. Most of the children there are indeed orphans," Lady Moreton said, looking a little confused.

"I do hope their mother will be able to take them again before too long," Mrs. Aldridge said. "Children belong with their mother, no matter what the situation."

"I would normally agree, ma'am, but in this case, I think the children are better off where they are," Lydia said. "I am planning on going again tomorrow and will be sure to check on them, though."

After this, general conversation resumed as normal and before too long the ladies excused themselves so the men could enjoy their port. When they joined them forty-five minutes later, Lady Welles announced the program for the rest of the evening, and Lydia's father escorted everyone into the music room in the back of the house.

Chapter Twenty-Nine

As they entered the music room, John noticed there were French doors leading out into a garden. They had been left ajar to allow fresh air to circulate in the room.

Lydia was just about to pass him to take a seat, but before she could, he reached out and grabbed her arm.

She gave a slight gasp of surprise.

"I'm sorry to startle you, but would you like to take a stroll with me in the garden?" he asked when she looked up at him curiously.

Her eyes shifted outside for a moment and then back to the guests who were still finding seats and chatting amongst themselves. "I don't know if that would be polite."

"Please? No one will notice us missing, I'm sure, and if they do"—he gave her a little smile—"we are newly engaged. I'm sure we will be forgiven taking the opportunity to spend a few minutes alone."

She gave a little giggle and then a nod before she allowed him to escort her outside.

They walked silently through the small garden, following a pathway that led through some pretty flower beds all a riot with daffodils and other spring flowers.

John wasn't entirely sure how to begin to vocalize the crazy mash-up of thoughts and feelings running through him. Finally, he simply took in a deep breath filled with the sweet scent of the flowers and began with what was at the forefront of his mind.

"I-I wanted to apologize," he started.

"For the other night?" Lydia asked.

"Yes, for the other night and the past few weeks when I persisted in thinking you something you are not. I knew you were hiding something, I just had no idea what it could be," he admitted.

"I don't understand why you jumped to the conclusion that I was stupid. Do you really believe all pretty girls have nothing in their heads?"

"No. I just—I had a bad experience once with some diamonds of the first water, and further experience with such girls hasn't done much to change my opinion. I understand it's expected that you'll gossip at parties, but sometimes I... Well, I don't know about *you*, but I find it all rather tedious after a while."

Lydia laughed. "Which is why you've caught me twice now having intellectual conversations with Lady Sorrell at parties."

He burst out laughing as well. "Of course! Of course. That makes so much sense!"

Their laughter died away as they came to the end of the garden. John leaned his back against the wall that delineated the Sheffield's garden from that of their neighbor's.

"And now, it seems as if I owe another apology," he said.

She cocked her head a little, waiting for him to elaborate.

"I thought you knew nothing of the poor, and it seems you not only know a great deal but have first-hand experience helping them."

"Ah, yes."

"But you never told me you were volunteering at the Dorothy School," he said.

She gave him a little smile. "I don't tell you everything I do, now do I?"

"No. I almost wish you would, though."

"You can't mean that," she said with a laugh.

"But I do. Not because I need to know what you're doing every day, but because... well, because I care. I'm interested." He stood up, away from the wall and took a step closer. He had to really work hard to restrain himself from taking her into his arms this very moment and crushing his lips to hers. No... No, he didn't want to crush anything. He wanted to kiss her. He wanted to feather his lips across hers until she opened that sweet, delicious mouth and let him inside. He wanted to taste her, to experience her, to get as close as two people could get.

She looked up at him, a soft smile lifting her beautiful, pink lips.

"The more I get to know you, Lydia, the sadder I am—"

She burst out laughing. "Getting to know me makes you sad?"

He gave a little chuckle. "Yes, yes it does. Because it means I know what I'm going to lose when you leave and that nearly devastates me."

The smile slipped from her face. "Oh," she breathed.

He couldn't resist. Not anymore. Not when she was looking so sweet and vulnerable.

He cradled her face in his hands and did exactly what he'd been dreaming of. She opened to him just as he'd hoped and tasted, my God, was it possible she could taste even sweeter than he had imagined?

He could taste the sweetness of the wine she'd drunk. He could taste the deliciousness that was just Lydia. And he wanted more, so much more. But he'd deliberately kept some space between them because he knew if he didn't he would be pressing himself against her, feeling her soft, womanly curves, wanting... Wanting so much more than he could ever have.

His heart was racing, and he could feel Lydia's pulse pounding in her neck. He needed to step away. He needed to stop. But she was so delicious. So wonderful. She was everything he'd ever wanted in a woman, in a wife.

But he couldn't have her.

He ended the kiss, resting his forehead against hers, breathing in her scent.

"I'm sorry," he said finally.

"Don't be." She looked up at him, her green eyes deep with passion, and something else—sorrow?

"I know you're going to be leaving. There's nothing I can do or say to change that." It was spoken as a fact, but he meant it as a question.

"No. There isn't. And I'm the one who's sorry."

"You won't—"

"Don't ask, please," she said, pulling further away both emotionally and physically.

He dropped his hands to his sides. "Right."

"We should get back," she said, turning away.

~June 8~

The children of the Dorothy School for Boys and Girls were twitching in their attempts to keep still as Lydia and Lady Moreton came in the following afternoon. Lydia nearly laughed at how excited they were, and she could hardly wait to share the fruit and other goodies she'd brought to supplement her mathematics lesson.

"Good afternoon, ladies," the matron said with a broad smile.

"Good afternoon, Matron, children," Lydia and Lady Moreton said together. They gave each other a look and laughed.

"We're so pleased to see you today," Lady Moreton continued.

"And we are very excited to have you here. As you see, today we have a slightly older group for you to spend time with. I hope that's all right?" the matron asked, raising her eyebrows a little.

"Oh, yes. I'm very happy to meet more of your students," Lydia said quickly.

"Most definitely. I brought books that will appeal to any age, I believe," Lady Moreton agreed.

"Excellent. I'm sorry Miss Hemshawe couldn't join you today," the matron said. It was clear that a number of the children agreed.

"Yes, sadly she couldn't make it," Lady Moreton said. She turned to the children. "Her father is very ill, so she is looking after him."

"We'll pray for him," one little boy said. The others all nodded wildly.

"That is so thoughtful of you!" Lydia said, impressed.

"I'm sure it will help him a great deal," Lady Moreton agreed.

"That is an excellent idea, Francis. Let's all take a moment to pray for his recovery," the matron said. She folded her hands in front of her body and bowed her head for a moment, closing her eyes. The children all mimicked her.

In her own mind, Lydia said a quick prayer for Diana as well.

After less than a minute, the matron opened her eyes and then split the group into two, sending half off with Lady Moreton to read stories and leaving the other half with Lydia to play her games. Half an hour later when all the food she'd brought with her was gone and the children's attention was beginning to wander, the matron came back into the room and dismissed the children to play outside in the courtyard for a brief time before they switched places with the other half of their group.

"Matron," Lydia said, getting up from the table where she'd been sitting with the children.

"Yes, Miss Sheffield, may I do something for you?"

"I was just wondering about the two children who were dropped off by their mother the last time I was here. What was the mother's name? Mary?"

"Oh, you mean Mary Small. Yes, her children are still here."

"Are they doing well? Getting acclimated? I do hope they're not missing their mother too much?" Lydia asked.

"Well, you are welcome to come see for yourself," the matron said.

Chapter Thirty

When Lydia gave her a nod, she led the way toward the back of the house where there were classrooms and an open drawing room for the children as well. The two little ones Lydia had seen being dropped off were there playing with the other children. Each seemed to be quite engaged in what he was doing. Lydia approached the older one, who couldn't have been more than five or six.

"Do you remember me?" she asked the boy.

He gave a little nod, his big brown eyes staring up at her.

"I was here when your mother left you in Matron's care."

He nodded again.

"I promised you that I would come to visit and see how you were doing. Are you happy here?" she asked the child.

"I miss me Mum, but Matron an' the misses are nice." He paused and then added, "An' the food's good."

Lydia gave him a big smile. "Good. I'm glad you're happy and doing well."

"If'n ye see my mum, tell 'er I miss 'er," the little boy said.

Lydia didn't know when or if she could ever see his mother, but she gave him a smile and caressed his head. "Of course I will, if I see her."

He accepted this and went back to his game.

"Thank you," she said to the matron. She wondered if John knew their mother. She would have to ask him some time.

~*~

John hadn't visited Mrs. Worthing, the proprietor of the secondhand clothing shop, for a number of weeks. He was definitely overdue to help her and her customers out.

Speaking with Lord Blakemore at the engagement party had reminded him of this sad fact, so he headed over to her store the afternoon after the party.

"Why, it's Mr. Welcome," she said with a chuckle when he came in the door of her shop.

He stopped just inside the door and laughed. "Mr. Welcome?"

"It's what they call you 'round here, didn't ye know?" the lady said.

"No, I didn't. Well, I suppose it's a lot better than some other things they could call me," he said with a laugh.

The woman guffawed at his joke.

"I'm certain there are some debts I could take care of for you today, Mrs. Worthing," John said, coming farther into the store.

"I'm certain there are," she agreed with a smile as she started toward the back of the store and her office.

John followed her in but stayed just inside the door. The room was hardly more than the size of a closet, and he didn't want to crowd her or make her feel uncomfortable. He waited patiently while she looked through her books and then did some calculations on a piece of scrap paper.

With their business concluded about fifteen minutes later, both moved back into the store proper with broad smiles on their faces.

"It is a pleasure doin' business with ye, sir," Mrs. Worthing said, straightening a pile of shirts on a shelf.

"And you, ma'am. I do hope your family is doing well?" he asked politely.

"Hale and hearty, sir, hale and hearty," she said with a huge grin.

John was lost in his own world, walking back to The Angel where he'd left his horse, when he nearly bumped into someone walking down the sidewalk a few minutes later. "I do beg your pardon," he said not even looking up.

"Ah, Lord Welles, well met," Mr. Meir said, giving John a nod.

"Mr. Meir! I'm terribly sorry. My mind was preoccupied, and I'm afraid I wasn't watching where I was going."

"Not a problem. Not a problem at all. I was wondering, my lord..." He paused.

"Yes?"

"If you'd rethought your decision from the last time we met, to, er, discontinue with our previous arrangement."

"Oh, no. I'm still determined to try other options, I'm afraid."

The man frowned, clearly not happy with John's answer. "I see. Well, then, good day to you."

He began to walk off with a determined step. John felt bad, but his desire to make Lydia happy was too strong. He knew it was probably misguided hope, but he wondered if it was his thieving that was driving her away. If he stopped, perhaps she would change her mind.

~June 9~

Lydia was enjoying a quiet afternoon reading through some texts her father had brought her on ancient Greek theatre. He'd been fortunate enough to attend Lord Pemberton-Howe's lecture. Sadly, he hadn't felt it was appropriate for Lydia herself to go, but he'd made it up to her by bringing her back these works for her to read through.

"I beg your pardon, Miss," said Michael the footman, coming into the study after a brief knock.

Lydia looked up from her reading.

"There is a gentleman here who says it's most important that he speak with you." He handed over a visiting card, but the name on it meant nothing to Lydia.

"Thank you, Michael. Please inform my maid and I'll be there directly."

"Very good, Miss," Michael said.

For a moment, Lydia sat there looking at the card in her hand, wondering who this man could possibly be. She wished her father were home and could see him with her. Sadly, he was off seeing to his own clients.

This fellow couldn't be one of her father's clients, could he? No, he'd asked specifically to see her. It just didn't make any sense that a complete stranger would come and ask to speak with her.

Well, there was only one way to find out who he was. Her maid would surely be waiting for her by now.

Polly followed Lydia into the drawing room and unobtrusively took a chair off to one side.

"Good afternoon. I'm Lydia Sheffield. How may I help you?" Lydia said as she came into the room.

The short, slender gentleman standing by the window turned and came forward to bow to her. He was a rather ordinary-looking man with brown hair and thick, round wire spectacles on his face distorting the size of his brown eyes. "Thank you so much for meeting me, Miss Sheffield. I hope I am not disturbing you. I promise I will take up as little of your time as possible."

"Of course. Please," she said, indicating the sofa and taking the chair opposite.

He settled himself in the center of the piece of furniture, but at the edge as if he needed to be ready to flee at any moment. "I am an, er, associate of your fiancé, Lord Welles."

"An associate?" Lydia asked. Not a friend. Not an acquaintance, but an associate. Whatever could that mean?

"Yes. I'm the person to whom he sells his, er, finds," he said, his eyes flicking over toward her maid. "Lord Welles has informed me that you were aware of his..."

"Hobby?" Lydia supplied. So that's who this man was. The fellow to whom John sold the diamonds he stole. But what could he possibly need to speak with her about? The question spun around in Lydia's mind, peaking her curiosity. She wanted so much to sit forward as he was, to show her interest in whatever he might say, but she also knew that she needed to remain calm and seem to be in perfect control of the situation. She didn't move a muscle but continued to sit back in her chair as if she weren't as anxious as she truly was.

He gave a little laugh. "Yes, you might call it that."

"I see. So, Lord Welles provides his finds to you and you pay him for them? Where do they go afterward—just out of curiosity?" she asked. Oh, she was good, remaining so calm, sounding as if meeting a gentleman who worked in illegal trade was an ordinary occurrence for her.

"To Amsterdam, where I have an associate," he said, giving her a little smile.

An associate who is a jeweler, she supposed, and could resell the pieces John stole. "I see. From your accent, may I assume you are also from Amsterdam?" she asked.

"Yes, indeed, I am. I don't suppose you've been?" he asked politely.

"Me? No." She gave a little laugh. "I've never been to the Continent."

"You should go some time. It is lovely."

She gave a polite nod. He was doing absolutely nothing so far to allay her curiosity. "I'm certain you didn't come simply to introduce yourself to me?" she asked, finally allowing it to get the better of her.

Chapter Thirty-One

Mr. Meir gave a little chuckle. "No." He sobered quickly, gave another brief glance at the maid, and then said, "I understand you've been encouraging his lordship to, er, discontinue his hobby."

Ah, so that was what this was about. Lydia gave the man a small smile. "Yes, I didn't feel it was appropriate behavior for a peer of the realm—or anyone, for that matter."

"I can understand that you feel that way, however, you do know there are a great number of people relying on his lordship continuing with this occupation."

So this was where John got that line he'd repeated to her innumerable times. Or maybe it was the other way around. Maybe John had said it so often to Mr. Meir that he had internalized the message himself. Well, she supposed, John had to justify his criminal activity to himself somehow.

"I do understand that, Mr. Meir, thank you. However, there are other, more proper ways of taking care of the problem," she pointed out.

"None will be so lucrative, I assure you."

"You don't know that—"

"Miss Sheffield, let me make myself perfectly clear, if Lord Welles discontinues this work the good people of the Rookeries *won't* be the only ones who will feel the pain."

Lydia sat up straighter in her chair. She'd almost jumped from it entirely, but managed to restrain herself at the last minute. "Are you threatening me, sir?"

From the corner of her eye, she could see Polly sit forward as well, ready to jump for help. Thank goodness she hadn't thought to meet with this man alone! Knowing Polly was there, and Michael was just outside the door, was very reassuring.

Mr. Meir gave a nervous little laugh and raised a hand. "No need for histrionics, Miss Sheffield."

Lydia swallowed her anger and forced her voice to remain light and pleasant. "I am not engaging in histrionics. If you want to see histrionics, I can most certainly show you some. However, I prefer to discuss this in a reasonable fashion. Now, answer me. Are you threatening me?"

He gave her a condescending smile as if she were a little girl testing to see just how hot the fire was. "I suppose you could take it that way. I *would* hate to see anything happen to either you or Lord Welles." He paused for effect. "However, I do know people who are capable of... Well, carrying out unpleasant tasks, shall we say?" He gave her a pleasant smile to belay the severity of his words.

Lydia narrowed her eyes and fought harder to contain her anger. It wasn't working. "Let me inform you, sir, that my father is a lawyer and my uncle a marquess. Should anything happen to me, things could get even more unpleasant for you than merely losing access to your supplier." She paused and then added, "May I make a suggestion, Mr. Meir? I believe it would be best if you returned to Amsterdam—immediately—and *stayed* there." She too paused, because two could play at that game. "If you have any difficulty in doing so, I know a good many people who would be more than happy to help you to remove yourself from London."

She stood before he could say anything further. "I believe it is time for you to take your leave, sir. Good day."

She turned her back on him and started to walk from the room, now so furious her hands were shaking and her heart was pounding in her chest.

"Are *you* threatening *me*, Miss Sheffield?" he asked incredulously, stopping her briefly.

She turned back and gave him her most pleasant, polite smile. "Yes, I am." With that, she walked out.

In the hall, she paused in front of Michael, grateful for once that her father employed such well-muscled footmen. "Throw the man in the drawing room out and don't be gentle about it." She then turned and stalked back to the study, Polly following on her heels.

"Miss," Polly whispered once they had entered the room. "Who was that man? And how dare he threaten you? My goodness, I'm positively trembling!" she said, lifting one of her hands to show how it shook.

"I'm sorry you had to witness that, Polly, although I am extremely grateful you were there," Lydia said. She then gave a little laugh and showed her maid that she was shaking too.

Polly took both of Lydia's hands in her own. It was almost reassuring to feel that her maid's were as clammy and cold as her own. "I *so* wish your father were here."

"I think we did all right without him," Lydia said, trying to give her maid her best reassuring smile.

"*You* did, Miss! My goodness, but you were so brave! You threatened him right back, you did!"

Lydia took a deep breath to try to calm herself and then gave another little laugh. "Yes, I did, didn't I?"

"I would never have been so strong."

"Well, I'm afraid I'm going to have to ask for your discretion, Polly. I don't think it would be a good idea if my father were to learn of this."

"But, Miss!"

"No, Polly. He doesn't know of Lord Welles' hobby and would be extremely upset if he learned any of what just occurred. I'm afraid... Well, someone *would*, in fact, get hurt—and that someone could just as easily be Lord Daniel. Do you understand?"

"But do you think this man will just return to Amsterdam like you told him?" Polly asked, her eyes going wide.

"I don't know. I can only hope he does."

"I don't think you should go out without a footman for some time, Miss. I would be right scared, if I were you."

Lydia gave Polly's hands a squeeze and then let go. "You may be right. I'll be careful, I promise."

~*~

John was shocked when his footman brought Mr. Meir's visiting card to him in his library that afternoon. The gentleman was asking for a minute of his time, the footman told him.

Never had Mr. Meir come to him before—and John didn't think he liked it.

"Show him in here," John told his man, getting up from his desk.

A minute later, the gentleman in question came in. He gave John a short bow and then came forward. "I'm afraid I have an extremely important matter to discuss with you, my lord."

"It had better be for you to come here," John said. It was one thing to carry on pleasant conversations with Mr. Meir at The Angel, quite another having him in his own home. Politeness, however, dictated he at least offer the man a seat. John took the wingback chair in front of the empty fireplace and indicated Mr. Meir sit in the one opposite.

The man sat at the edge of the chair. "You need to do something about your fiancée," Mr. Meir said, getting straight to the point. "She has just threatened me."

John jumped from his chair. To hell with niceties. "What? How did you meet her? Where?" Did Lydia seek him out or did he seek her? He wouldn't put it past that girl to go into the Rookeries—alone—and find his associate.

Mr. Meir stood as well. "I admit, I went to her home—"

"You went to see *her*?" John's anger spiked. Not only had this man invaded his private home, but he had been to see Lydia? This didn't mean Lydia was no longer the object of John's anger—she had obviously seen the man and spoken with him.

"I went to ask that she encourage you to continue with our business arrangement," Mr. Meir continued, ignoring John's outburst. "I wanted to inform her that whatever she might plan in order to raise funds for the good people of the Rookeries, it won't nearly be as much as what you earn from me."

"You dared to go to the home of my fiancée in order to use her influence on me?" John could not believe the nerve of this man.

"I dared because she is threatening years of work. She is trying to stop you from carrying out your good mission," the man said. He was clearly upset as well. He could not be thinking straight to have done something so bold. So stupid. So utterly outside the confines of their relationship.

"That is *my* problem, not yours. You had no right—"

"Well, let me tell you, sir, that while I was as polite as could be, she threatened me. Yes! Threatened me!"

Chapter Thirty-Two

"So you said earlier. And how *did* such a sweet, gentle young woman threaten you?" John asked, crossing his arms, his initial anger cooled significantly at the thought of his laughing, smiling, charming Lydia threatening anyone. It was almost funny.

"She told me to leave the country—immediately. And she reminded me that her father is a lawyer and her uncle a marquess—facts you seem to have forgotten to mention to me." He frowned fiercely at John, his oversized eyes staring at him hard. The man was clearly deranged.

"That's because it is none of your business who Miss Sheffield's family is. Never did I imagine you would ever have an opportunity to encounter her."

"Well, I have and I am affronted. No, not just affronted, I am leaving. I have come to inform you of the boldness of this woman you have associated yourself with and recommend you put her aside immediately. No man should have to deal with such a harridan."

"*Harridan?*" Never in his life could John even imagine Lydia as such. He would have laughed except for one thing that had caught his attention. "Wait, you are leaving?"

"Yes. She threatened to have me *removed* from the country. I would prefer to do so on my own terms, albeit, rather sooner than I had originally planned."

"But you'll be back in a few months, as usual," John said, just to be sure.

"No, I will not. Our association is at an end, sir."

John opened his mouth to say something, but he had nothing to say. Lydia had threatened this man. Told him to leave and never return—and he was going to do so. John's anger returned with force. "And you are going to take the threats of a young woman seriously?" The man might be deranged, but John still needed him. Lydia had yet to come up with an idea to replace his current method of raising money. He was not simply going to walk away from everything he had done because Lydia didn't like it, because she threatened his only contact to the underworld of jewelry thievery.

"Considering who her family is?" Mr. Meir said, his overly large eyes going wide. "Considering that her father is a *lawyer*? Considering that she is clearly too intelligent for her own good?"

"But you had to have known..."

"I knew nothing of who she was until she informed me," the man admitted.

John narrowed his own eyes at the man in disbelief. "You *knew* that I'd become engaged."

"I had heard as much," he agreed. "And I figured your fiancée was the daughter of a peer. But you and I both know society is full of useless men who father equally silly girls. I would suggest you look in that direction for a wife, my lord. Someone who will provide you with children and be a pleasant life-companion, not this... This conniving, controlling creature to whom you have affianced yourself."

John forcefully kept his jaw from dropping open.

"So, to answer your question, yes, I most certainly *am* letting her threats dictate my present-day actions and my future plans. Good day, sir, and good bye." Mr. Meir turned and walked out of the room.

John couldn't believe it. His one and only way to earn money to support the people of the Rookeries was going to leave and there was nothing he could about it.

And it was all Lydia's fault!

She had told Meir to leave. Threatened him! How could she? How could she destroy John's life in this way?

Well, he was not going to take this as easily as Mr. Meir had. He was not about to dance to her tune.

John stormed out of the house.

A quarter of an hour later, a cab dropped him off outside the Sheffield home. He knocked on the door and then barged in straight past the footman who answered. "I need to speak with Miss Sheffield immediately, where is she?"

"In her private parlor taking tea, my lord," the man answered.

"Upstairs?" John asked. He'd never actually been to Lydia's private room before.

"Yes, I could—"

"I'll find it," John said, starting up the stairs.

"Please, my lord, allow me," the footman said, chasing after him.

He passed John at the top of the stairs and then knocked before opening the door at the end of the hallway. "Miss Sheffield, Lord Welles—" And that was all he had a chance to say before John pushed past him.

"Just what the hell do you think you're doing threatening people?" John said as he walked into the room.

Lydia was seated on a pretty, pale green sofa very like the one in his mother's room. It was situated in front of the fireplace on the wall that cojoined with the house next door. She lowered her teacup from her lips. "I beg your pardon?"

"I have just been visited by Mr. Meir at my *home*." John hoped his meaning that this was unusual was getting through. Lydia looked much too calm for John's satisfaction.

"He went to see you? Just now?" she asked, still holding her cup ready to drink from it.

"Yes. He never comes to my home, but he was upset because he had just been threatened—by *you*." He crossed his arms and widened his stance as he glared at her.

She stood as well, after replacing her cup carefully in its saucer. "And did he inform you that I only did so after he had come *here* and threatened not only *my* well-being but *yours* as well?"

John frowned. "He threatened you, physically?" Meir had not mentioned this "minor" fact earlier.

"He said he knew people who were available to carry out '*unpleasant tasks*'. And said that the people of the Rookeries weren't the only ones who would feel pain if you stopped selling him the diamonds you stole."

For the second time that day, John's mouth dropped open. He couldn't believe Meir had threatened Lydia! If he weren't so furious with her, he'd run out and threaten the man himself. "And so, in response, you destroyed any chance that I could ever do business with him again."

"Yes, I did. I will *not* be threatened, John."

"My God, Lydia! I would never want you threatened either, but I rely on him to buy those diamonds. Without him, I'll never be able to support the people who are counting on me."

"I told you, we'll find another way."

"Yes, so you say. But you've also said that after the season is over you're going back to your precious life up north. You're going to leave me. You won't *be* here to raise money. How am I going to support these people after you leave?"

She looked at him as if she hadn't thought of this little wrinkle in her plans. "Just because I'm not here doesn't mean—"

"Yes, it does. I'm not going to carry out whatever strange plans you might have had. I can't do that. I had a perfectly good way of supporting these people and you just destroyed it."

She stood there silent.

"So was this your plan all along?" His hand fisted in frustrated anger. He wouldn't have noticed except for the pain as his nails dug into his palm. "From the moment you caught me with my hand in the Emmerton's safe, was this your plan? First you threaten me, then *force* me to fall in love with you, all with the express purpose of breaking my heart when you leave to return to your own life in the north of England. And now you've made it so I can't even support the people I've sworn to help—my life's work. And all this without *any* sort of explanation as to why you won't marry me. Why you're going to leave. Why..." John clamped his mouth shut and swallowed hard. "The *least* you can do, now that you've completely ruined my life and plan on breaking my heart, is to tell me why."

It was Lydia's turn to open her mouth and close it again without saying anything. She turned her face away, toward the fireplace.

"Well?" he growled, coming another step closer.

"I-I'm scared," she said so quietly he almost didn't hear her. "I'm scared of dying."

"Dying? What are you talking about?" Did she think Meir would actually have her killed? If so, she was even more of an idiot—

"Childbirth. My mother died in childbirth. I'm scared I would as well. The only way to avoid doing so is to not become with child. The only way to do that is to not marry." She turned back toward him, tears streaming down her softly flushed cheeks. "That's why I can't marry you. I—"

"My God, Lydia," another voice whispered from the direction of the door.

John spun around to see Lord Daniel standing there looking as if he might start to cry as well.

"Papa! What are you... How long have you been there?" she asked, swiping away the tears from her cheeks.

"Long enough—no, too long." He looked at John. "You and I are going to have a little talk after this, Welles."

Lord Daniel came farther into the room and took Lydia's hands in his. "I am so sorry, Lydia. Why did you never tell me about this?"

"About my fear of childbirth?" She gave a sound that was half cry-half laugh.

"Yes! This is my fault. It's all my fault. I never... I could never discuss your mother's death with you. It was too raw and painful right after it happened, and then, well, it seemed as if you had gotten over it. But you never did, did you?"

"How *could* I? I saw her die, Papa. I saw her bleed to death right in front me," she said, tears started to stream down her face once again.

He pulled her into his arms. "I know. I'm so sorry, baby. I'm so, so very sorry." He rested his cheek on top of her head, his own eyes glassy with unshed tears. "I wish you had said something to me. I wish I had said something to you, but you always seemed so happy."

"Because Mama told me to be. The very last thing she said to me was 'Be happy, Lydia.'" She began to cry in earnest, then, and even John had trouble keeping his own eyes as dry as he might wish.

He quickly blinked them away, however, and took a deep breath to steady himself.

"Of course she wanted you to be happy. She loved you. And I love you," Lord Daniel said softly. "But she wouldn't have wanted you to fear childbirth or to never marry because of that fear. Please, Lydia, don't ruin your own life because of what happened to your mother."

"I can't... I can't help it, Papa. I can't do it," Lydia said. She pulled away from her father and turned to John. "I'm sorry, but I truly can't marry you." And with that, she ran out of the room.

John heard a door slam down the hall a moment later.

He turned back to her father. He felt bad for the man, but perhaps not bad enough. "I'm sorry, my lord, but I wouldn't marry her now even if she didn't have this fear. She's destroyed me."

"Oh, I beg to differ. She may have put an end to your illicit activities, but you *will* marry her."

CHAPTER THIRTY-THREE

John followed Lord Daniel down to his study. It was odd, but he saw the room with new eyes now that he knew how intelligent Lydia was.

The pile of papers and books on the center table that John had assumed were Lord Daniel's, he now wondered if they were hers. He took a glance at one pamphlet that sat closed on the table. It was written by Lord Pemberton-Howe on his findings in Greece. Yes, that had to be hers. John shook his head, hardly able to believe what an idiot he'd been to think her stupid.

But now wasn't the time to reprimand himself for that. He had much more serious things to worry about. He took a seat on the sofa across from Lydia's father.

They sat in silence for one full, very uncomfortable minute.

"How long have you been getting away with this?" Lord Daniel finally asked.

John raised his eyes to look at him. "Nearly three years. At times I've left a calling card—the Jack of Diamonds."

Lord Daniel's mouth dropped open slightly and his eyes widened. "You're the Jack of Diamonds? The Watch have been looking for you for years!"

"Yes, I know."

"You must be very good," Lord Daniel said, almost to himself.

John stayed quiet. Now was not the time to brag about his ability to hide in plain sight, nor slip a piece of jewelry off a woman's person without her even being aware of it.

Lord Daniel sighed and then rubbed a hand over his face. "Look, you're a peer of the realm. They're not going to try you in court."

"I know."

"They expect men such as you to have a stronger moral compass," Lord Daniel said pointedly.

"It is for a good purpose," John said, finally defending himself.

"Right. Because you're some Robin Hood, now, are you?"

John had nothing to say to that. He did think of himself that way.

"Look, I know what your father did—selling what he could—"

"He sold everything and anything of value on our property, down to the crops in the ground," John said, trying to contain the anger he still felt at his father's lack of foresight. "If he had only left the crops, left the farm and the animals, I wouldn't be in this position. I would still be able to earn money to live and more to support others... But there's nothing there. Nothing left."

"Your mother said you're slowly working on rebuilding," Lord Daniel said.

John nodded. "I take a very small amount from what I get for the diamonds to invest in my estate. I'm hoping that in ten years or so, it will be back to where it was before my father stripped it bare."

Lydia's father nodded his approval. "There's more that you can do."

John looked up again.

"To help the poor. And it will help not just the people of the Rookeries, but people throughout the country. Take your seat in Parliament. Fight for them there. Propose legislation."

John sat back. He'd never considered becoming a politician. He didn't know if he would be any good at it.

"Lydia would be the perfect political wife, you know. She's intelligent, clever, and charming. She would be able to lobby for you among the women and probably the men as well."

John nodded slowly. Lord Daniel was absolutely right. "If I do that..." John started.

"I won't have to threaten you, and frankly, I think you've had enough threats for one day," Lord Daniel said, a small smile playing on his lips.

"What do you mean, threaten me?"

"Well, I was considering saying that if you didn't marry my daughter, I'd turn you in to the authorities and destroy your reputation—since that is all that would happen if I did so. But I think you're going to do the right thing." He paused to let John think about that for a moment. "You are a good man, John. I would be proud to call you my son-in-law, but you've got to stop stealing. Don't stop supporting the people you care for—I'm not asking you to do that. Just go about it in another way. And if you can help even more people, well, why wouldn't you?"

John nodded. "All my life, I've looked up to my father," he said quietly. "I've watched him do everything he could to help the poor. But he never once took his seat in Parliament nor even considered it—and neither did I."

"Why do you think that is?" Lord Daniel asked. "The idea had to have occurred to him."

John just shook his head. "He was shy. Painfully shy. My sister's the same way. She can't stand going out in public. I thought I was the same way, in fact, until I got to university and made friends. We would come down to London and attend parties. It was the most fun I'd ever had. I really enjoyed it."

Lord Daniel smiled. "So you're more like your mother in that respect?"

John smiled. "Yes, I suppose I am."

"Then instead of following in your father's footsteps—or Robin Hood's—I would suggest you create a path for yourself."

John could only nod. It was excellent advice.

"And figure out how to get Lydia to marry you, because when you told her that you loved her, I don't think she actually comprehended what you said. I'm certain she's in love with you—she just may not realize it yet because her fear has been clouding her judgement. Help her get past that, and I think you'll find yourself a very happy man."

~*~

Lydia was cried out by the time her father came tapping at her door. She'd cried too many tears for her mother already, she wasn't sure she even had any more.

"Lydia?" her father poked his head around the door.

She was sitting up on her bed, a handkerchief in one hand, a pillow tucked up under her chin. "Come in, Papa."

He came and sat on the edge of her bed. "He loves you, you know," he said, giving her a little smile.

"I know. He said so."

Her father gave a little laugh. "He said you forced him to fall in love with him. I liked that."

She couldn't help but smile. "As if I could ever *force* anyone to do that."

"I think you did it unintentionally. He couldn't help but fall in love with you. You're beautiful, funny, and charming."

"Did he say that or you?"

Her father shrugged. "I did, but I'm sure he'd agree."

She rested her cheek on the pillow snuggled up against her chest.

"Why did you never tell me you were afraid of dying like your mother did?" he asked softly.

"How could I?" she asked, lifting her head again.

"I don't know. You might have tried discussing it with me. Mentioning to me?"

"And what would you have said—'No, Lydia, don't be silly. That won't happen to you'?"

He gave her a little smile. "Probably."

"I've heard that before. It doesn't help. You know why?"

He shook his head.

"Because you don't know that. You don't know that I won't die in childbirth. I'm sure Mama never realized that she would."

"She knew it was a possibility. There's always the possibility," her father said quietly.

Lydia frowned at her father. "Is that supposed to make me want to do this?"

He laughed softly. "No, not really. It's just the truth. But it doesn't mean you shouldn't get married. You never know, maybe you won't even conceive."

She just looked at her father disbelievingly.

"I don't like the fact that you lied to me, Lydia," her father said, becoming serious again. "You lied to me about this fear and you lied to me about being happy. You lied to me about this engagement, which you went into fully intending to break off at the end of the season."

She straightened the cover on her pillow, smoothing down the soft, white cotton, and not looking at her father. She felt bad for lying to him and had certainly never meant to hurt him in any way, but what else was she supposed to have done?

"Please, promise me that you won't do that anymore? If you're sad, tell me. If you need someone to talk to, I'm here. Hey..." He put a finger under her chin and lifted her head so she was forced to look at him. "I love you, Lydia. And just like your mother, I want you to be happy. But you don't have to pretend, all right?"

She gave a nod.

"Now what about Welles?" he asked.

"What about him?"

"Do you love him?"

She gave a nod. She hadn't been one hundred percent certain before, but she was now. She'd known that she liked him a great deal. She'd known that she enjoyed spending time with him and admired his dedication to helping the poor—

misguided thought it was in the way he chose to do so. But he was clever and kind and thoughtful, and she was now absolutely certain if there was any man in the world for her, it was John Welles.

"And you don't think you could put aside your fear for him?" her father asked softly.

She shook her head. "I've thought about it, but it's just..." She sighed. "It's not worth it, Papa. I'm not ready to sacrifice my life, not even for John."

"So, that it's it then? You're not even going to try to get him back?" her father asked.

She looked up at him again, feeling the tears well in her eyes once more. "I don't know if I could," she said, although her voice wasn't working quite right, and it came out more as a whisper. "I don't know if I *should*. It's not really fair to him. I'm sure he wants children. He's a viscount. He needs an heir. But I can't give it to him."

"Well, you can..."

"I won't."

"Think about this, Lydia. Don't make any decisions just yet, all right?" her father said before he left her to her thoughts once again.

Chapter Thirty-Four

Lydia had entertained the idea of not going to her Whist Society meeting for approximately ten seconds. Yes, it was true she wasn't feeling in top form and hadn't been since she had stormed out of the parlor after telling John and her father her secret, but that didn't mean that she should punish herself. She'd had a full day to recover and wallow in her sadness. A day of company might just make her feel better.

She enjoyed the weekly card games. She enjoyed the camaraderie and the gossip, although she could have done without the constant bickering between the Duchess of Kendell and Mrs. Aldridge. But she had a feeling everyone felt that way. She just didn't understand why those two ladies could not get along.

Lady Norman always did a good job of making sure they didn't end up at the same table, however, without it ever being obvious. Today, Lydia was partnering with Lady Sorrell, and Mrs. Aldridge with Lady Blakemore at the same table.

"You're being very quiet today, Miss Sheffield," Mrs. Aldridge said, giving her a sidelong glance over her cards.

"I apologize. I'm afraid I've got quite a bit on my mind."

"Anything you'd like to share?" Lady Sorrell asked, looking up from her own cards.

"No, I..." Lydia unfanned her cards and put them facedown on the table. "Maybe I should."

"You know we'd be more than happy to help with any sort of problems you might be having," Mrs. Aldridge said, placing a warm hand on top of Lydia's.

"Thank you, Mrs. Aldridge. That is very kind of you. It's, it's a matter of the heart, I'm afraid," Lydia said with a smile.

"Is something wrong with your relationship with Lord Welles?" Lady Blakemore asked, becoming quite concerned.

Lydia gave a little nod. "I'm afraid I did something the other day that has made him quite furious with me."

"Oh, dear!" Mrs. Aldridge said, now folding together her own cards.

"It doesn't have to do with our little conversations, does it?" Lady Sorrell asked.

Lydia gave a little laugh. "No. He's discovered that I was telling him the truth when he asked what we'd been discussing."

"What were you discussing?" Lady Blakemore asked, looking for Lydia to Lady Sorrell.

"And where?" Mrs. Aldridge added.

"The use of the chorus in ancient Greek theatre at Lady Wrexley's soiree a few weeks ago," Lady Sorrell said. "But when Lord Welles joined us, we quickly changed the subject to something innocuous because, apparently, Lord Welles didn't believe that Miss Sheffield had the intelligence to be discussing anything of an academic nature." She gave a little laugh at the ridiculousness of the situation.

"He has since learned the error of his ways," Lydia said. "But no, this is different. He's... He's been working with a gentleman to help the poor of the Rookeries," she said, trying her hardest not to give anything away that shouldn't be known. "And I'm afraid I offended the gentleman, and he's now refusing to work with Lord Welles anymore. As you can imagine, my fiancé is not happy with me." She lowered her eyes as they began to sting with tears. "He says I've destroyed his life."

"My goodness! That's rather hyperbolic, isn't it?" Lady Sorrell asked.

"You might think so," Lydia admitted. "But helping these people truly was his life's work. He is very devoted to them, and now I've made it impossible for him to continue to support them in the way he had been before."

"But surely there are many ways to help people?" Mrs. Aldridge said.

"He needs to raise money, but I'm not exactly certain how to do so," Lydia said.

"What? Raising money to help the poor? It's the easiest thing in the world," Lady Blakemore said with a little laugh.

"But how?" Lydia asked.

"Well, you could simply ask people to donate to the cause," Mrs. Aldridge suggest. "Goodness knows I've been asked a great many times for money."

"Or we could hold a party and require everyone who attended to pay an admission price with the money going to the cause," Lady Blakemore offered.

"Or, we could have a whist party where all of the winnings go to the cause," Lady Sorrell suggested.

Lydia gasped in delight. "A whist party? What an absolutely brilliant idea!"

"What's that?" Lady Norman said from the other table. "Is there going to be a whist party?"

"Yes, to raise money to support the poor of the Rookeries. Lord Welles's people," Lady Sorrell said, turning around to speak to her.

"What a wonderful idea!" Lady Moreton said.

"I would most definitely be interested in participating," the duchess said.

"Could we... would you very much mind if we planned out how such a party would work and who we might invite?" Lydia asked, getting up, her own game of whist completely forgotten. "Lady Norman, do you have any paper I could use to make notes?"

"Of course!" the lady said.

"Oh, and I'd like a piece please. I think Lord Welles should be informed of our idea as well," Lady Sorrell said, turning and giving Lydia a wink.

"Do you think..." Lydia started, feeling her heart begin to pound ever so slightly.

"I believe he should be given the option to join us, don't you?" the lady asked with a broad smile.

"You see, your problem is solved, Miss Sheffield," Mrs. Aldridge said with a broad smile. "All you needed to do was share it with us, and it is taken care of, easy as getting wet on a rainy day."

"You are all quite amazing," Lydia said, feeling truly grateful.

"What was the problem?" Lady Norman asked, coming back with paper, pens, and ink.

"There was a misunderstanding between Miss Sheffield and Lord Welles, but this party that we're planning should take care of it. And...perhaps a whisper of an apology in his ear?" Mrs. Aldridge said with a significant lift of her eyebrows.

"Most definitely," Lydia agreed.

~*~

John was enjoying a moment of quiet in his study when the footman came in with a note on a salver. He'd been trying to work, but his mind was still churning with all of his problems. His book was open, his pens and paper were at the ready, and yet he sat there not reading, not making notes, not doing anything but thinking.

"This just came for you, my lord. There's a man waiting for an answer," his footman said.

His curiosity piqued, John picked up the note and read it. His presence was being requested at Lady Norman's home immediately. Lydia's name was invoked, but it was unclear whether she was in trouble or what the issue was beyond that he was asked to come.

He looked up at the footman, who was waiting patiently for his response. "Please have Lady Norman informed that I will be there directly."

"Yes, my lord." The footman went off to deliver the message.

He closed up his book, and carefully put away his pen, ink, and paper. He had no idea what was going on, but he was determined to find out and, if possible, have a private word with Lydia—not that he knew what he would say to the girl. He still hadn't come to any conclusions about how he felt or what he was going to do about marrying her. Maybe inspiration would strike in the moment. It was all he could hope for.

All the ladies of the Whist Society were present and working with great animation when he arrived. There was some laughter, some arguments, and Lydia sitting and writing furiously as a few other women dictated something to her.

"Ah, Lord Welles," Lady Norman said as he was announced. All of the women stopped what they were doing to stand and curtsy or nod to him, depending on their station. He bowed to them all collectively. "Welcome," she said. "As you can see we are all very busy, but we felt it was important you were made aware of what we were doing."

He gave her a nod. "I thank you. What is it you all are working on?"

"A party," Lady Moreton answered with a smile.

"A whist party," Lady Sorrell added.

"To raise money for your people," Mrs. Aldridge said.

"My people?" John asked. Who were his people?

"The people you support in the Rookeries," Lady Blakemore said.

Little paws climbed up his leg and John realized a small black and white dog with long floppy ears and an impressively fringed, furiously wagging tail was trying to get his attention.

"Duchess, down!" Mrs. Aldridge barked. "I beg your pardon, my lord."

"Oh, er, no problem." He reached down and gave the dog a little pat on its head. He nearly commented on the fact that the lady had called the dog Duchess, but one look at the Duchess of Kendell, and he decided to hold his tongue. This was obviously something of contention between the ladies. He refocused on what the ladies had just said. "Do I understand you correctly? You're organizing a whist party to raise funds for the people of the Rookeries?"

"Yes, that's it," Lady Blakemore said. She turned to Lydia and added, "He is not lacking in understanding. I see no reason why you can't work things out."

Chapter Thirty-Five

Lydia flushed a little and stole a glance up at John from under her eyelashes. She cleared her throat. "I did say, my lord, that we would find a way to replace your other source of income."

"And you think this will make up for it?" he asked, completely unconvinced that this would, in fact, do what she thought it would.

"Yes. I envision this would earn—what did you say earlier, Mrs. Aldridge? We would charge each person a fee to come in and then take fifteen percent—or did we decide on twenty-five percent—of each person's winnings?" Lydia said.

"Twenty-five," Lady Moreton supplied.

"Yes, so at the very least we would earn a thousand pounds simply on entrance fees, and then however much people wagered and won," Lydia explained.

"You will most likely end up with at least twenty thousand, if not much more. And that's simply the first party. We can, naturally, make this recurring event," Mrs. Aldridge said.

"And we were thinking we might get some of the gentlemen's gambling clubs involved and ask them to suggest that gentlemen donate a percentage of their winnings there one evening, again on a recurring basis," Lady Normal said.

"And I was going to suggest people at the horse races I attend do the same," Miss Hemshawe added.

"We're talking a lot of money here, my lord," the duchess said. "Certainly, enough to support a number of families for years, if not longer."

"My goodness, I am…impressed, ladies," John said, slightly overwhelmed.

"It was most definitely a group effort," Lydia said.

John nodded.

"Er, might we have a word—in private?" Lydia asked with some hesitation in her voice.

"Yes. Yes, of course. I would like that," John said.

The other ladies gave Lydia either a knowing smile or a word of encouragement before she led him into the game room next door. Strangely, she moved to the wall farthest away from the drawing room despite there were no chairs there.

"That wall opens," she said quietly, nodding toward the wall between this room and the drawing room. "I imagine that sound carries through it very easily."

He gave a little laugh. "I see," he said, keeping his own voice low.

"Perhaps it would be better if we held this conversation in the privacy of my home, but… But I think I need to say this now while I have the nerve. I hope you'll excuse me."

He gave her an encouraging smile, hoping whatever she was about to say would make his life easier. She was either going to tell him she'd changed her mind about her fear, about marrying him or, well... He supposed he should simply wait for her to tell him what she had to say.

She took in a deep breath. "I wanted to apologize," she started.

"For what? There are any number of things which you might apologize for," he pointed out.

She winced. "I know." Briefly, she closed her eyes. "First, I want to address your relationship with Mr. Meir. I won't apologize for threatening him because he threatened me—and you. Our safety."

John shook his head. "He should not have done so."

"No. He shouldn't. I will not allow anyone to threaten me or you in that way," she said seriously. "And while you know I don't approve of your..." Her eyes strayed to the wall separating the two rooms. "Hobby," she finished discreetly, just in case anyone could over hear their conversation. "As promised, I have found an alternative."

"And one that can continue without your presence being necessary," he pointed out as the thought suddenly occurred to him.

"Yes." Her gaze dropped to the floor so he couldn't see her eyes. Was she pleased about this? Conflicted? Sad? He couldn't tell.

"And I wanted to apologize for not telling you about my...fear sooner. I should have told you sooner you."

"It's a rather personal thing," he said. "I understand you wouldn't want to discuss it freely."

"Indeed."

"Your father still thinks we should marry," he added, hoping she might have an answer to this dilemma.

She gave him a little smile. "My father has great hopes."

John could only laugh at this. "Hopes that we'll marry or that you'll somehow be able get beyond this fear?"

"Both, I suppose."

"What do you think?"

"I don't know. I wish I did. I'm going to have to reflect on this further. But for the time being, I'm asking for your patience, and...your friendship. Is it too much to ask?" she said, looking up at him with uncertainty.

She looked so beautiful. So vulnerable. How could a man say no to those eyes? He could only smile.

She reached out her hands. He took them and gave her a gentle squeeze of reassurance. He would stand by her. He would wait until she had made up her mind, until she had figured out what she wanted to and what she could do. He truly had no other choice.

~*~

Daniel was happily finished with his work for the day. Three clients seen to, two of their cases happily resolved. There wasn't much more he could do for his third case. The law just wasn't with the client.

As it was merely four o'clock in the afternoon, he decided to stop at Hatchard's bookshop and see if they had anything new that might interest either him or Lydia. He'd just walked in when he noticed Lady Norman looking through a display of novels.

"Lady Norman, I hope you are doing well," he said, walking up to her.

She turned and gave him a smile and a little curtsy. "Very well, my lord. And you?"

He bowed. "The same. Is there anything interesting that's new?"

"Oh, quite a bit!" She giggled.

He looked at her with a small smile on his lips. "I meant amongst the novels, but perhaps there's something else even more interesting?"

The lady's smile grew. "We had our society meeting today, I'm sure you're aware," she began.

"Ah, yes. It's Wednesday."

"Yes. Miss Sheffield was kind enough to entrust us with a small problem she was having with Lord Welles. I'm sure you must be aware of it? Something having to do with his ability to help people?" She looked at him to be sure he was following. Of course he understood immediately what she was referring to, but it was evident she was vague on the details.

He was certain Lydia was the cause of her lack of complete understanding of the particulars and was grateful for his daughter's discretion. "Yes, I know of it. Were you able to assist her in some way?"

"We spent over an hour planning a whist party to raise funds," she said triumphantly. "It's going to be the hit of the season, I'm sure!"

Daniel widened his eyes. "A whist party?"

"Yes. Everyone who attends will pay an entrance fee and then we'll collect twenty-five percent of the winnings from the games played," she explained.

"Brilliant!" he said, very impressed with their ingenuity.

"And, not only that, I sent a note to Lord Welles and asked him to join us in our planning. He did so and spent a good quarter of an hour or more speaking privately with your daughter. They seemed to be on much better terms after that." The lady looked very pleased with her matchmaking skills.

"I am exceedingly happy to hear this," he said.

"I thought you might be." She gave him a big smile and then added, "Now perhaps you might have need to go and visit with Lady Welles?"

"To tell her the good news?" he asked, not quite sure what she was hinting at.

"That, and perhaps to speak to her about a more personal matter between the two of you? Oh, don't think for a minute that I, and some of the other ladies of the Whist Society present at your dinner party last week, didn't notice you and Lady Welles seemed to have a, er, *close* relationship?"

Daniel caught his mouth from dropping open. "There is nothing formal between us," he began hesitantly.

"Oh, no, I would not expect there to be until your children are settled. But now, perhaps…" She allowed him to finish her thought in his own mind.

Yes, now, perhaps, if Lydia and John had worked things out between them, he *should* go and settle things with Ann. It would be wonderful if he could do so.

Chapter Thirty-Six

John finished telling his mother about the fund-raiser the ladies of the Whist Society were putting together as they enjoyed their dinner. He was so grateful his mother seemed to be fully recovered now.

"But that's wonderful!" his mother said, taking a sip of her wine. "John, you do know what this means, don't you?"

"That there's hope I'll be able to continue to support the people who rely on me? I think that was the point, Mother," he said with a laugh.

She gave him a momentary scowl, but it didn't last long before it was replaced by a broad smile. "No, silly, it means that Lydia loves you and wants to be with you."

Sadly, John lost his own smile. "I don't know that's the case. I asked her if she had any hopes of us actually getting married, and she said that she didn't know. She was still thinking it through."

"Naturally, she needs a little bit of time to come to terms with her newly discovered feelings, but she *does* love you. Of that I'm certain."

John shook his head. "I'm not convinced. I believe it means she's thinking about it, just as she said."

"And what are *you* going to do about it?" she asked, setting aside her fork. She still wasn't eating enough, in John's opinion.

"I'm going to wait, I suppose. And help you to another serving?" he asked, picking up the platter with the meat on it.

She held up her hand. "No, thank you, I'm full. Do you really think waiting will get you want you want?"

"I'm not even convinced marrying Lydia *is* what I want," he said, beginning to let his frustration show. The platter hit the table harder than he had intended it to.

"You love her?" his mother asked.

"Yes, of course I do!" He took a large gulp of his wine.

"Then you want to marry her," she said, as if it were the most obvious thing.

"But after what she did with Mr. Meir..."

"She was being threatened! Do you really want to marry a girl who can't stand up for herself? Who simply allows others to walk all over her? I didn't think you were that sort of man."

"No! Of course I don't. But she didn't need to destroy my business dealings with him," he argued back.

"I honestly don't see that she had a choice."

"No, not when she didn't approve of my arrangement to begin with."

His mother just sat there looking at him expectantly.

"And I don't like being threatened by Lord Daniel either. I will *not* be forced into marrying Lydia!" he added forcefully.

"Even if it means doing exactly what you want to do?" she asked quietly.

John refilled his glass of wine and then his mother's. As he put down the decanter, he sighed. "I'm behaving like a child, aren't I?"

His mother didn't say anything. She just took another sip of her wine.

John could only shake his head. "I love her. I want to spend the rest of my life with her. But I also want to have children with her. What can I do about that?"

"I don't know," his mother said. "But the first step is getting her to want to marry you. From where I stand, I don't believe you've done very much to persuade her in that direction."

"I've danced with her. Gone to parties and been social with her, just as she asked," he said.

"That was weeks ago. What have you done recently? And what have you done that she hasn't specifically *asked* you to do?"

John thought about it, but in all honesty, he didn't need to. He knew the answer as well as his mother did. Nothing. He'd done nothing to win Lydia's affection. He hadn't needed to until now.

"I heard about a small theatrical group who will be performing Antigone at a theatre not too far from here tomorrow night," he said, thinking this through.

His mother sat back. "And what has that got to do with anything we've been discussing?"

He gave her a little smile. "Lydia loves Greek theatre."

"Aahhh." His mother gave him a huge grin. "That's my boy."

~June 12~

John picked up Lydia the following evening in his mother's carriage.

"Are you going to tell me where we're going or are you going to keep it a surprise until we get there?" she asked as he handed her up into it.

"It's going to be a surprise," he said. "But I do appreciate your trust and confidence."

"Well, I am bringing my maid."

"I noticed," he said with a laugh.

"One can never be too careful when going out with men," she said with a mischievous twinkle in her eye.

"Indeed, but I think you'll be pleasantly surprised by what I have in store."

When they arrived at the theatre, John found their way to the small box overlooking the stage. The theatre was rather sparsely attended with the area in front of the stage looking much emptier than Lydia had ever seen at a theatre. It was also a much smaller theatre than the one she usually attended with her father.

"I don't know this theatre," she commented, taking her seat.

"As you can see, not a great many people do. But I'm hoping the players and the program will make up for that," John said, sitting beside her.

"Are you going to tell me what play it is?"

"No. I think I'll let you figure it out for yourself," he said. He couldn't hold back the grin on his face—and couldn't wait until she figured it out for herself. The anticipation was almost as enjoyable as he hoped the play would be.

Lydia gave him a playful frown and then turned to watch as the stage lights were lit.

"Ismene, dear sister," a woman said, walking onto the stage wearing a peplos, the traditional ancient Greek woman's dress. "You would think we had already suffered enough for the curse on Oedipus. I cannot imagine any grief that you and I have not gone through. And now—have they told you of the new decree of our King Creon?"

Lydia gasped and clapped her hands quietly. "It's Antigone! You brought me to see Antigone!" she whispered loudly to John. Her face was aglow with excitement as the play continued on.

John could only laugh and nod.

They watched with rapt attention, not saying a word, until the intermission. Lydia had not only been silent, but had hardly moved a muscle throughout. She seemed transfixed by the action before them.

When the players left the stage at the end of the act, John stood and stretched, but before he could move much more than that, he was attacked by a grateful Lydia.

"You are truly the most wonderful man, John Welles!" she said, beaming up at him.

"Well, the acting isn't very good, and I'm extremely uncertain about this translation of the text," he began.

"I don't care about any of that. You brought me to see Antigone!" Lydia giggled.

Chapter Thirty-Seven

The rest of the evening sped by as the play came to its expected tragic end. They chatted about it on the drive back, but before they reached her home, John paused and took Lydia's hands in his own.

"Lydia, do you know why I wanted to take you to see Antigone this evening?" he asked, softening his voice.

"Because you knew I would enjoy it? And you were so right! Oh, thank you, John. It was truly wonderful," she said, giving his hands a squeeze.

"I *did* hope you would like it, but I did because... Because what I said to you the other day after you saw Mr. Meir is still true." He gave a little laugh. "You may have missed it, you were so upset at the time."

"I didn't miss it," she said, smiling shyly at him. "You said I forced you to fall in love with me." She gave a little giggle. "As if I could ever *force* you do to such a thing!"

"You may not have done it intentionally, but, well, just by being who you are, I couldn't help it. I do love you, Lydia, and I want to make you happy." He paused, feeling his heart pounding in his chest. This was probably the hardest thing he'd ever done—

actually proposing, seriously proposing to a woman, and meaning it with all his heart and soul.

Oh, he'd done so lightheartedly before, but somehow now, this time, it seemed so much more real. More serious.

"Lydia, will you make me happy by saying that you'll marry me?" he asked.

Her eyes began to shine with unshed tears. She blinked a few times to clear them. "You've asked me this before," she pointed out.

"I know. But this time... This time I truly want you to say yes and mean it."

She gave a little laugh. "Because my father threatened you, otherwise?"

"No! No, not at all." John let go of her hands feeling a little frustrated. "Lydia, I just told you, I love you. No matter what your father said or did, it doesn't matter. All you need to think about and consider, please, is that I love you and I *truly* want to spend the rest of my life with you."

Lydia's gaze dropped to the seat in between them. "I love you too," she said quietly.

The words were hardly out of her mouth when John reacted, not even thinking, not even trying to restrain himself. He grabbed her and kissed her with all his love and passion.

He'd only just started to show her just how much he loved her when he felt her pressing against his chest, pushing him away. He loosened his hold on her.

"You didn't let me finish." She giggled. "I love you too, but I *can't* marry you. You *know* this, John. You know my fears. You've got to understand. It's not you and it's not anything else. *You* are wonderful. It's *me*!"

"Lydia, you can't ruin your life for this fear," he argued.

"I can because I want to *have* a life. I don't want to die," she said, her eyes turning glassy again.

"So few women die in childbirth, Lydia. You don't know you will be one of them—"

"John, which would you rather—having me as a friend for twenty or thirty years, or having me as a wife for one?"

They had reached her home. The door next to her was opened before John could even respond to her query. He could only sit there and watch her get out and disappear into her house. Never in his life had he felt so empty.

~June 13~

Lydia didn't want to be the cause of speculation and gossip, so she dutifully presented herself at the Shropshire's ball the following evening. She wore one of her more flattering gowns, one that her friend Tina had made for her before she'd stopped being a modiste and entered society. Just wearing this dress always made Lydia feel good. It was the palest green with white lace trim and made her cheeks look pink even when she was certain they were much more pale than usual.

It took more effort than usual to put on her mask of happiness that evening—to laugh and smile and tell funny stories. It was expected, however. If she didn't, then those tongues would wag and all eyes would turn to John—if he were present.

So far, she had yet to see the man who was still, technically, her fiancé. She wasn't quite sure how she was going to face him—not after what had happened the previous night. She wondered if he would be able to tell she had spent the rest of that night alternately weeping into her pillow and kicking herself for being such a scared idiot.

She wanted so much to be able to tell him that she would marry him. She wanted so much to truly be happy. But visions of a blood-soaked bed and her pale, waxy-looking mother kept flashing before eyes. She knew that would be her if she married him, and frankly, she still had too much to live for and nothing to die for. Certainly not some tiny blue baby which had never even taken a breath of life for which his mother had given her own.

No, she just couldn't do it.

"A moment of quiet for the ever-smiling Miss Sheffield? How could this be? What could you possibly have on your mind?" John's voice broke Lydia out from her momentary reverie.

She turned a smiling face toward him. "Nothing. Nothing at all. How are you this evening, my lord?"

"I am well, thank you. Might you be willing to join me in this dance?" he asked, bowing before her and holding out his hand.

She placed hers in it, while curtsying. "I would love to dance." She gave a little giggle, her mask firmly back in place as she allowed him to lead her onto the floor.

~*~

"I can't believe you talked me into coming tonight, my lord," Ann said, looking up at Daniel with a broad smile.

"I believe it's good for you to get out more. Now that you are fully recovered from your illness and fully out of mourning, it's important you show yourself to society," he answered, itching to take her hand in his. He knew he could not actually touch her, as he so wanted to do, but merely had to content himself with her company for the evening.

"And why do you think that?" she asked.

"It's good practice, don't you think? Once John and Lydia are married…" he started.

"Won't you be returning to your home in the north?"

"I will," he agreed. "I've got a business there. Clients who are depending on me and so on."

"And I—"

"I'm hoping you will be with me," he said, cutting her off. "I know this isn't the right place for such a declaration, but I don't think what I'm going to say is going to come as a surprise."

"Do you think we dare even discuss such a thing before the children are settled?" she asked.

Daniel turned to watch his daughter laugh at something John said as they executed the steps of the country dance. "I think we might."

Ann turned to watch them too, her smile returning to her face. "Well, in that case, I think I may need to pay a visit to my modiste so that I can update my wardrobe. This dress was the closest thing I had to the current styles," she said, indicating the deep purple silk gown she was wearing.

"I think you might want to do that," he said, giving her a wink. "Although society in Doncaster is rather sparse, you may be called upon to entertain quite a bit. I didn't know how to teach Lydia how to organize a party, so we didn't entertain often. Now, however, I'm hoping you'll be able to make up for so many years of quiet living."

"Well, I will do my best," she said with a little giggle.

~*~

After her dance with John, Lydia sought out the lady's retiring room to have a slight bit of torn lace repaired on the hem of her dress. Her attention had wandered for just a few minutes during the dance, and she'd not moved precisely when she should have. The woman next to her had moved and accidentally trod on her gown. Both of them had been horribly embarrassed, but these things happened at times.

Lydia was standing, still allowing a maid to stitch up her dress when two ladies came in, chatting away.

"When does Peter get home from school for the holidays?" one woman was asking her friend. They were both well-dressed ladies about ten years older than Lydia.

"He's already home," the second woman said with a scowl. "Got sent down a few weeks ago. Wild behavior, the headmaster called it."

"Oh dear," the first woman said, clucking her tongue.

"He's been taking fences he shouldn't when he rides and taunting the other boys for riding more carefully. I just don't know what to do. It's his father's fault, I'm sure of it," the second one said, clearly unhappy.

The first woman laughed. "I remember when Francis went through a phase like that. He thought he was invincible—until he got thrown by his mare that refused to jump a fence at the last minute. I can tell you being laid up in bed for a month with a broken leg cured him right up."

"Well, the only broken bones Peter is going to suffer are the ones I inflict on him if he doesn't stop this nonsense. My younger ones are starting to mimic him, and I don't like it," the second woman said.

"There you are, Miss," the maid said, recapturing Lydia's attention.

"Oh, thank you," Lydia said and handed her a coin from her reticule. With her dress repaired, she had no reason to stay in the room with the gossiping women. Peter's mother had seemed unhappy with her son, but in a strangely fond way despite her threat to break his bones. Lydia didn't know what it was that made her think that, and it really didn't make any sense to her. How could a woman be fond of a child who misbehaves and threatens his own well-being? Well, at least one thing was perfectly clear, both of them had survived childbirth, at least once. For that they must be very grateful.

Chapter Thirty-Eight

Lydia told herself that she was merely continuing to keep up pretenses when she accepted an invitation from John for a drive two days later.

"It's a lovely day," she said, settling herself beside him on the bench of his phaeton.

"It is," he agreed, giving her a smile. "But then, any day I spend with you is a lovely day."

She giggled and shook her head. "You are quite the charmer when you want to be, my lord."

"You know I've come to realize you don't actually know me quite as well as you might think you do," he said as he navigated the streets on their way to the park.

"Oh? Are you going to share some of your secrets with me?" she asked curiously. That would be quite a turnaround.

"Nothing as momentous as yours, I'm afraid. Merely that, yes, I can be quite charming when I want to be. I can also be quite stubborn. When I want something, I will not quit until I get it."

"I think I knew that about you. I have to say, I've never met anyone more determined than you to persist in helping people, even when you don't have the means to do so. Honestly, most men would have simply thrown their hands up in the air and said they didn't have the funds. But not you, my lord. No, you simply found another way around the problem."

"Not a completely honest one, but yes, I did," he agreed with a pleased grin. "But I was referring to something else."

"Oh?"

"You," he said shortly, before turning into the park.

"Me? What about me?"

"I want you, and I am determined to have you—as my wife. And stop your protests right there, Lydia," he said, cutting off anything she might have been about to say. "I know you don't want to have children. And although it would sadden me greatly, I've decided I would be willing to forego having any, for you."

Lydia was speechless. She could only look up at John, sitting next to her with a small smile playing on his lips, as he settled his equipage into the slow crawl that was the daily drive down Rotten Row.

"You would do that for me?" she said, finally getting her voice to work past the lump in her throat.

"I would. And I've been, er, making some discreet inquiries into exactly how one might ensure that one *doesn't* procreate. It's not fail-proof, but I think we could manage it." His cheeks turned slightly pink at the indelicate turn the conversation had taken.

Lydia, for her part, was still so overcome with the thought he would be willing to forego having an heir for his title and estate that she didn't even care. But then, his words penetrated her happy fog. "It's not fail-proof? You mean that we *might* conceive?"

"There is much less likelihood that we would, but yes, there is no way to ensure that you don't unless we completely abstain, naturally."

"Of course, which is why I decided that I would never marry," Lydia pointed out.

"But you love me and I love you. We want to spend the rest of our lives together. This is a way to do it."

"No, John, it's not. If there is the chance that I could... I'm sorry, but I'm not willing to take that risk. It's just not worth it." She turned back toward the front. After a moment she said, "Oh, look, there is Mrs. Aldridge with her son and Lord Ainsby."

"What's not worth it?" John asked, his voice straining to stay calm. "Me? Am I not worth it?"

Lydia could feel tears begin to prick at her eyes, but she was not going to cry in public! Instead, she laughed as if he'd just said something amusing. "Oh, John, you are worth a great deal to me, but are you worth my life? Are you worth a dead child?"

He paled. His voice was quiet when he finally spoke. "There are a great many more children born with no complications than otherwise. There are many, many more who live."

It was true. She knew it was true. But *could* she take the risk?

~*~

Early that evening, John paid a visit to Mr. Cartwright, paying him from funds left over from the last time he'd sold a batch of diamonds to Mr. Meir. He wondered when the ladies were going to hold their whist party. It couldn't be too long from now; the season was going to be over in another month.

They concluded their business quickly and then John commented, "I'm surprised Timmy isn't here playing as he usually is. And Mrs. Cartwright? Is she well?"

The man pulled his ledger close to his chest. "She's well. She's looking after Timmy. He's... he's not..."

"Is he not well?" John filled in when the man didn't seem capable of continuing.

"Measles, we think," the man said, paling slightly. He was clearly extremely upset.

"I'm so sorry to hear it. Could I visit with him? I brought a few pastries, and he enjoys them so much," John said, giving him what he hoped was an encouraging smile.

"That's very good of ye, sir. Very good. Let me just take a peek in and see if the missus thinks it's awright."

"Of course."

He waited a few minutes, hearing muted whispers in the other room. Mrs. Cartwright came out with her husband.

"I'm so sorry to hear Timmy's not feeling well," he said after greeting the woman who was doing in her best not to look as if the world was coming to an end.

"Oh, God bless ye, sir. No, he's not. Right worried we are too." She led the way into the other room where the boy looked tiny in a mass of blankets on a narrow bed shoved into the far corner. A larger bed stood next to it and a clothes press stood nearby. The room wasn't quite large enough for the amount of furniture in it.

John took the chair just next to the child. He seemed to be sleeping fitfully. Red, nasty spots covered his face and arms. It did indeed look like the measles. He just hoped it wasn't something worse.

"Hey, Timmy," his mother nudged him as she sat down on the edge of the bed.

When the boy's eyes fluttered open, she said, "Look who's here to visit ye. It's Mr. Welles."

John smiled down at the child. "I brought you some tarts. I hope you're hungry."

Timmy gave John a little smile, but shook his head. "Not hungry," he croaked. "Mummy, you eat them for me."

His mother tsked. "Now, now, you need to be polite and eat what Mr. Welles has brought you." She looked at John and said quietly, "Hasn't had a thing for nearly two days."

"Look here, Timmy," John said as he plucked a tart from the packet he'd brought. "It's apple. Your favorite, isn't it?"

The boy gave a little nod then struggled to sit up. His mother reached out to help him up and adjust the pillows behind him.

The boy took the tart and gave a tentative little bite. He chewed reluctantly and swallowed, before handing the tart over to his mother. His little eyes closed, and within a moment, he was fast asleep again.

John gave his head a little caress and then helped him to lie flat again. "He tried. That's good enough."

"I'm that sorry, sir," Mrs. Cartwright said.

"No, no. I'm sorry he's feeling so poorly. If he's not better in another day or so, please contact me."

She gave a nod and led John back to the door. "You heard about Mary Small, then?" she said as they went.

"I heard she had to leave her children at the Dorothy School," John said with a nod.

"It's because she's doing poorly herself," Mrs. Cartwright said.

"Really? I thought it was a matter of money," he said, turning around to face the kindly woman.

"That too. But there might be problems with the babe."

John widened his eyes. "That's not good. Is there a doctor?"

"Ugh, not in these parts," the woman shook her head.

"I'll see what I can do about that."

"It would be that wonderful if ye could," she said, a smile gracing her face for the first time since he'd come in.

He needed to think about this, but surely there was someone on whom he could call to see the woman. He, of course, would pay any charges. The problem would be finding someone who would venture into this part of town.

CHAPTER THIRTY-NINE

~June 16~

John was at a loss. He had tried everything he could think of to entice Lydia to marry him, even offering to forego having his own heir, which had not been easy. He was giving her a few days to think things over. Hopefully, she would change her mind. He wondered if he should ask his mother to have a word with her. Perhaps talking about it with another woman would be helpful.

On top of this difficult situation, there was still Mary Small and little Timmy Cartwright, both of whom needed to see a doctor. Well, that, he thought ruefully, he could do something about. For that problem, there was an answer.

He just needed to find a physician.

But where did one find someone willing to go into the most dangerous area of London in order to attend to patients who had no possible way to compensate them? John didn't have a great deal of money left from what Mr. Meir had given him for the last delivery of diamonds. He'd given away the bulk of it and sent the rest to his steward to pay for supplies necessary to rebuild the farm on his estate. He hoped he had enough to pay someone the exorbitant rate any physician would surely charge for such a visit.

The trick was finding such a man.

There was only one place where John had any hope of doing so—Powell's. John shoved aside everything else in his mind and went out.

The gaming room was crowded as always. In fact, John had never seen it otherwise. He searched around for Lord Wickford, the owner of the club, but didn't see him anywhere. It only left John with one option, join a game and ask around.

There were three men John vaguely knew playing vingt-et-un at a table toward the back of the room. "Mind if I join?" John asked, coming up to the last empty chair.

"No, not at all. Welles, isn't it?" one of the men asked.

"Yes." John sat down and pulled out a handful of coins he'd brought with him.

"Wrexley," the man said.

"Ah, right. I had the pleasure of attending your wife's soiree last week."

"My apologies. I have to admit, I spent the night here." The man laughed.

"Can't stand to attend your own parties?" one of the other men said, laughing along with him.

"Ugh! No! The wife insists on throwing them every so often but with the full knowledge that I won't be there. It's a nice little arrangement we have. I let her throw her parties, and she lets me not attend."

John smiled. "It was actually a very pleasant evening."

"Well, I'm glad you enjoyed it." Wrexley dealt out the cards and the men got down to serious play.

After a little bit, John ventured to ask the table at large. "You don't happen to know a physician, would you?"

"Eh? Feeling poorly?" one of the other men asked.

"No! Not me. Someone I know," John said.

"Oh, no. I don't know any. You, Wrexley?" the man asked, turning to the other man.

"No. They're all quacks if you ask me. Ask Wickford, he's bound to know. He knows just about everything," Lord Wrexley said.

"I was going to do that, but I didn't see him here this evening," John admitted.

"In the reading room," the third gentleman said. It was the first thing he'd said all evening and came out more like a grunt.

"Ah! I didn't think to look there. Thank you. I think I'll just finish this hand, then, and go in search of him. Rather important that I find someone, you know?"

The men all nodded, and they finished up quickly so John could find their host.

John hadn't actually spent much time in the club's reading room. If he wanted to read, he did it at home. But he understood that for some gentlemen, it was more pleasant to escape and come somewhere quieter or where the only company was male.

Lord Wickford was sitting and having a drink and a quiet conversation with another gentleman when John spied him.

"Good evening," John said to the men.

"Good evening," Wickford said, standing up. "You know, I don't believe I've ever seen you in here before, Welles. Normally you prefer the gaming room." He smiled at John. "Is there something you needed from me?"

"I'm sorry to be so obvious, but yes. Might we have a word? It won't take above a few minutes," John said with a smile to the other man. The fellow nodded amenably.

"Of course. Not a problem. You'll excuse me?" Lord Wickford said to his friend.

He led John over to the side of the room where few people were about. "What can I do for you?" he asked.

"I'm looking for a physician," John started.

Lord Wickford took a small step back.

John laughed. "Not for myself. For, er, someone I know. A woman."

"Oh! I see," Wickford said meaningfully.

"No, no! It's not like that. Not at all. She's simply someone I know." John knew that he wasn't explaining himself very well. "I, er, do some work in the Rookeries. Helping people. She's one of them and I've heard she's not feeling well."

"Ah. I understand now," Wickford gave John a warm smile. "I might have actually heard of your work. You aren't the man they call Mr. Welcome, now, are you?"

John's mouth dropped open a touch in surprise. "How did you know that?"

Wickford laughed. "I hear things." He winked. "Do a little work in the area myself."

"Really? I'm very happy to hear that!" John said earnestly.

"There are, unfortunately, a good number of people who need our help there."

"Yes, indeed, there are. Have you heard of a woman named Mary Small?"

"No. I've not met her," Wickford said.

"No matter. She's a very sweet thing. Her husband left her with two little ones and another on the way about six months ago. She's recently given her two children to the Dorothy School because she can no longer care for them, and now I hear she's having difficulty with the third—as yet unborn."

"I am sorry to hear that. So you're looking for someone who might be willing to venture into that part of town and possibly even work for free, then?"

"I'll pay him. I just... Well, it would be appreciated if he didn't charge too—"

"Of course! Someone who won't cost you three cows and a goat," Wickford said with a smile.

John laughed. "Yes, I suppose you could put it that way."

"I actually know just the man you need, and he might not even charge you a farthing."

"Really?"

"And, on top of that, from what I hear, he's an excellent doctor up on all the latest techniques and what-not," Wickford said, warming to his subject.

"And he won't charge anything? Who is this paragon and where can I find him?" John asked with a laugh.

"I was just speaking with him. Come, I'll introduce you."

~June 17~

"Miss, Lord Welles is here to see you," Michael said, coming into the study where Lydia was re-reading Antigone. She'd started it the day after John had taken her to see the play performed and was still working at it. The Greek was slow going, but it was well worth the effort.

She finished a note she'd been taking and then looked up. "Oh! How lovely. Take him to my sitting room. I'll be there in a moment."

Michael bowed and went off to do as she'd asked.

A few minutes later, she entered the room to find John staring into the empty fireplace.

"I hope everything is well," she said, coming up to him when he didn't look up at her entrance.

"Oh, yes," he said, his lips stretching into a smile upon seeing her. "I'm sorry, I was just lost in thought for a moment."

"Yes, so you seemed. Come, have a seat. Shall I call for some tea?" she asked, sitting in a chair on one side of the fireplace.

"No, thank you. Actually, I was wondering if you'd be interested in coming with me to meet Mary Small this afternoon," he said, sitting at the edge of the sofa.

"You're going to see her?"

"Yes, and since you know her children, I was thinking that hearing about them from you might cheer her up. I've heard she isn't doing very well, sadly."

"Oh, dear! Do you know what's wrong?"

"No. But I've got a doctor who's going to meet me there in about half an hour. Would you care to come with me?"

Lydia thought about those poor children she'd met at the orphanage and remembered how upset their mother had seemed when she'd left them there. "Yes, thank you," she said. "I would like to meet her.

I spoke with her older child when I was last at the orphanage.”

He nodded and gave her a smile. “I’m sure she’d love to hear what he had to say.”

“I’ll just get a wrap and be right with you,” she said.

Chapter Forty

They made inconsequential small talk on the drive there, for which Lydia was grateful. The closer they got, the more nervous she became. She'd never been to the Rookeries before and didn't know what to expect. She'd seen the homes of some of her students in Doncaster but had never visited the home of someone who wasn't of her own class here in London.

It was clear John hadn't visited Mrs. Small before this either. Oddly enough, this made Lydia feel better. She didn't know what she would have thought if he had. She honestly didn't know what sort of woman Mary Small was. Before they descended from the carriage, she stopped John. "Is Mrs. Small a...a...woman of loose morals?" she asked, not quite certain how to phrase it.

"No. As far as I know. I believe she worked for a florist before she had to quit her job. She is truly married—or was. Her husband disappeared about six months ago."

"Oh! How awful!"

"Indeed. Are you ready?" he asked gently.

"Yes. Yes, I believe I am. Thank you." Lydia allowed him to help her from the carriage and then followed him to a dark doorway just across the street. His knock elicited no response. After a minute, he simply tried the door. It was open.

He glanced back at Lydia before taking her hand. "Stay close. I'm not certain why this door is open nor why Mary isn't answering it."

Then went in and immediately up a steep flight of stairs, which were lit only by the soft glow coming from the room at the top. They emerged into a good-sized room. There was a table against one wall, a well-worn dark blue sofa on another, and in the corner, a large bed on which a woman sat panting.

"Oh, thank goodness you're here. I need some help," a gentleman in his shirtsleeves said from the head of the bed where he'd been wiping the woman's forehead with a cloth.

The woman grunted and groaned and seemed to be straining and crying all once.

"What, what's wrong with her?" Lydia asked, trying her best to keep her voice steady but failing miserably.

"Wrong? Nothing. She's giving birth," the man said.

Lydia immediately turned around to leave. She couldn't stay here. Not with a woman giving birth! She couldn't watch that again. My God, she couldn't watch someone else die!

John grabbed her arms and held her steady. "It's all right. The doctor is here. It'll be fine."

"No. No! The doctor was there the day my mother—"

"Lord Welles," the doctor said from the woman's side. "Please, I need help."

"Yes, of course. What can we do for you?" John said, pulling Lydia closer to the bed.

The room stank with sweat from the woman. The closer Lydia got, the stronger the smell became. Her mother hadn't smelled so, she remembered. She'd been clean and cleaned regularly throughout the entire process. Lydia supposed that was one difference between the wealthy and the poor.

"I need one of you to hold Mary's hand, the other to wipe her with this cloth, that's all, I'll do the rest," the doctor said. He handed the cloth to Lydia and showed her the bowl of water that sat on the floor just next to the bed. She had no choice. She *had* to help.

She bent down and rinsed out the cloth with cool water, taking in a deep breath before sitting at the edge of the bed. "There, there, now," she said as calmly as she could, "it's all right. It's going to be all right."

"That's a girl," John said encouragingly. Lydia didn't know if he were talking to her or Mrs. Small, but it was reassuring in any case.

The woman lay back, panting. Her eyes fluttered open. "Do I know ye?" she asked.

"We haven't actually met, but I saw you when you left your children at the orphanage," Lydia said. "My name is Lydia."

Mrs. Small nodded. "I remember ye were there. Are ye a teacher at the school?"

"No. I just go there to help out sometimes. I saw your children the last time I was there," she said, thinking that a conversation might be a nice distraction from the pain she was clearly feeling.

The woman gave her a little smile. Her crooked teeth were remarkably white, and her smile lit up her whole face so that she was almost pretty.

Lydia used the cloth to brush back the dirty blonde hair from her forehead where it stuck with sweat.

"How are they? Mickey and Mark?"

"Are those their names? You know, I asked your son, but he was a little shy."

Mrs. Small gave a little laugh. "Yeah, he's the quiet one."

"But he did say he and Mickey were happy there, and indeed, they seemed to be so," Lydia said.

"Ah, that's goooo..." Her word changed into a grunt of effort as she suddenly strained forward.

"That's good, Mary, good," the doctor said from the bottom of the bed. "If you want to push, you go right ahead."

For the next few minutes, the woman did nothing but grunt and groan with effort. She then flopped back onto her pillow, panting.

"Good! The baby's head is nearly there. Just a little more pushing, and we'll have him," the doctor said encouragingly.

Lydia took advantage of Mary sitting back to wipe her forehead and the back of her neck.

She opened her eyes and looked up at both her and John. "Yer so good to me. Thank yeeee..." And so it started once again, less than a minute after the last one ended.

The doctor gave more encouragement, and Mary let out quite a scream, making the hair on Lydia's arms stand straight up. She, herself, had to work from keeping her hands from shaking as she rinsed out the cloth and reapplied it to Mrs. Small's forehead.

"That's it, we've got the head. Now for the difficult part—the shoulders," the doctor said, giving them a smile.

That wasn't the difficult part, Lydia thought. She bit her tongue, ensuring she didn't utter a sound of dismay. Strangely enough, Mrs. Small didn't seem at all surprised by this pronouncement.

Another ten minutes later, with a lot of screaming, grunting, and groaning, the doctor gave a little whoop. "That's it. That's it. The shoulders are out aaand..." He drew the word out as he worked on something. "Here she is! A beautiful baby girl." He held up a squirming, slimy, screaming child, it's umbilical cord still attached to her mother. "Lydia, is it?" the doctor said.

"Yes," Lydia said.

"Come here and bring that blanket." He nodded to a folded piece of cotton draped over a chair nearby that Lydia had taken for a gown.

She handed the cloth to John and fetched the blanket as instructed. The doctor carefully placed the baby into it as she held it out to him.

"Oh!" She hadn't expected to be handed the baby! She'd never held a baby before.

"Come now, Mary, one last push and you're through," the doctor said.

Lydia stopped paying attention to everything but the child screaming in her hands. She was beautiful and disgusting and fascinating all at once. She just couldn't stop staring. Her attention was pulled away, however, when the doctor cut the baby's cord and, with a few efficient stitches sewed it off.

"There now, you can hand her over to her mother," the doctor said.

"What? Oh, yes, of course." With amazement, Lydia carried the baby to Mrs. Small, who was sitting there with a big smile on her face. She was still coated in sweat and panting, but she held her arms out for her child and then cooed over her happily as she screamed in her arms.

She put her smallest finger in her mouth and gazed adoringly at her as she began to suck at it. "Oooh, she's a strong one," she said with a little laugh. "I've been wantin' a girl, seein' as I already have two boys."

Lydia was confused. She looked back at the doctor, who was standing there smiling and wiping his hands clean on another cloth. She turned and looked at Mrs. Small again. The woman seemed to be in her own little world of joy, holding her new infant in her arms.

John stood up, smiling. "That was incredible, doctor," he said.

"The miracle of birth," he said with a nod, the smile not faltering from his face.

"Is-is Mrs. Small going to be all right, then?"

"Oh, yes, she's just fine," the doctor said. "Mary, do you have someone who can come and look in on you?" he asked her.

"Agh, yeah, my neighbor Patty, will come if'n I ask," Mary said, not even looking up from the baby as she continued to suck on her finger.

"How about if I give a knock on her door and ask her to come and look in on you later on this evening?" the doctor asked.

"Hmmm-humm," Mary said, not even paying him any attention.

He just laughed.

"And that's all? She isn't bleeding or...or..." Lydia asked just to be certain.

"No. She's fine. She needs to get cleaned up, but I think we can leave that to her and the neighbor." He pulled his coat back on saying, "I'll just pop next door and see to that."

Lydia could hardly take her eyes off the mother and child. Just a few minutes ago, Mrs. Small was nothing but a moderately pretty woman with crooked teeth who smelled. Now she was... She was glowing. She was beautiful. And it was all because of the child in her arms. Lydia could see that clear as day. She'd watched the transformation happen before her very eyes and still couldn't believe it.

Mary Small had not only survived childbirth, but her baby had as well. Never had Lydia ever seen anyone so happy as Mrs. Small was right now.

"The pain..." Lydia began, still not able to take her eyes off the mother and child.

For the briefest moment, Mrs. Small looked up at her, a beatific smile on her face. "It's all worth it for this, ain't it?"

Chapter Forty-One

Lydia was silent all the way back to her father's house. John had asked Lord Colburne to take a look in on little Timmy Cartwright, and he'd been happy enough to do so. What was even more amazing was he'd declined any sort of payment. John hadn't anticipated that.

"My pleasure," the man had said when John had offered a second time to pay him for his time. "I like to support those in need. Call me anytime."

John could only thank him and then join Lydia in the carriage.

"Are you all right?" he asked as they neared her home.

"Yes," she said quietly, not turning from the window. When she did, she looked at him silently for a moment. "I think I need some refreshment after that. Would you like to come in and join me?"

He nodded. "I'd like that."

It wasn't too much longer before they were comfortably ensconced in her sitting room, each with a glass in their hand. Lydia had been kind enough to send for some port for him in addition to the Madeira for herself.

"Well, a toast to Mary's new baby, then?" he said, raising his glass.

She laughed. "To the newest little Small."

He burst out laughing. "Indeed!"

"It was an incredible experience," she said after taking a sip of her wine.

"It was. Not at all what I'd been expecting, I have to say."

"Well, no. How could you?"

"If I'd realized she was that close to her time, I wouldn't have asked you to come—or indeed, have gone myself."

"But you didn't know," Lydia said.

"No. All I'd heard was that she wasn't feeling well."

"It was good of you to find a doctor to see her," she said, clearly relaxing a bit with her wine.

He gave a little shrug. "It was easy enough."

"She looked so happy...after."

"Like the Madonna she was named after," he said with a smile. He'd been awed by the woman's transformation. One moment she'd been screaming and clutching onto his fingers so hard he feared she would break them, and not two minutes later, she was a completely different person with her baby in her arms.

He'd noted Lydia's expression as well when she'd held the baby before passing it onto its mother. She was in awe. There was no other word for it but that. Complete and utter awe.

They sat in silence, each lost in their own thoughts for a few minutes, before Lydia said quietly, "It's worth it."

"I'm sorry?"

"That's what Mrs. Small said. She looked up at me and said it was worth it. All the pain and...and whatever else. It was all worth it just to hold that child in her arms."

John could only smile and nod—and pray that Lydia might be having a change of heart.

"I... I think I might want that," she said, her eyes beginning to shine with tears. She blinked but one slipped out and slowly made its way down her cheek.

John put down his glass and joined Lydia on the sofa. He wiped away her tear with his thumb. "You don't have to."

She shook her head. "But you yourself said there's no way to be sure that I wouldn't..."

"No. There isn't. Not if we consummated the marriage," he agreed.

"And I... I would like to do that," she said quietly. She looked up at him, her eyes still shining. "I love you, John Welles, and I... I think I'd like to have a child with you. I want to feel that...that... Whatever it was that Mary was clearly feeling. I want to create a life."

Before his heart could burst out of his chest with joy, he pulled Lydia close and held her there.

EPILOGUE

The Duchess of Kendell was sharing the sofa in the home of Lady Ayres, formerly Lady Norman, with Mrs. Aldridge. Lydia was so happy to see them. Not only were the two of them sitting, happily chatting away, but Mrs. Aldridge's dog, Duchess, was sitting in the duchess's lap! If she hadn't seen the two of them make up two years ago, she would never have believed it possible.

"Lydia!" Diana said, jumping up from a chair.

The other women all turned toward the door where she stood holding her baby in her arms. Within a minute, she was surrounded by happy, cooing women all trying to get a peek of little Johnny.

"Oh, he's beautiful," Lady Ayres said.

"Blond, like his father," Mrs. Aldridge said approvingly.

"And those eyes, so green, like his mother's," the duchess agreed.

Lydia was so happy to be back with her friends. It had been too long—a full year during which John would hardly let her out of his sight. He'd had a physician in every single month of her pregnancy to check on her and then more frequently as her time got closer. She couldn't have asked for better care or a more loving, attentive husband.

With minimal fuss, John, his mother by her side, and her father pacing the hallway outside her door, Lydia had managed to have her little Johnny and finally knew that feeling of bliss she'd seen that day on the face of Mary Small. Now, she understood what it meant to be a mother, and she was so glad she'd decided to put aside her fears. She didn't think she could be happier—except maybe when she would provide a sibling for little Johnny.

Author's Note

Thank you so much for reading Jack of Diamonds, the second book in the Ladies' Wagering Whist Society. Each of the books of this series feature a member of the society with either that lady or a relative of hers as one of the protagonists—either the hero or heroine.

Before I begin to write each story, to get to know my main characters better, I frequently write a short story explaining their backstory or an important episode in that characters' life. These stories I publish in my newsletter, which goes out on the fifteen of each month to those who sign up to receive it. If you'd like to do so, please click here or go to my website, meredithbond.com, to sign up.

Just to give you a taste, and so that you can get to know John Welles a little better, turn the page to find his story which I sent out to my dedicated readers.

Enjoy!

Merry

Diamonds of the First Water

Fate and a random room assignment brought John, Sebastian, and Mark together. John, the heir to a viscountcy and Mark, the Earl of Thetford, had gone to Eaton together. Sebastian, Marquess of Cenway and heir to a dukedom had been raised on the continent, but he was quickly making up for that by using his excellent language skill to attract the ladies, which was, after all, the best use of such knowledge.

Mark might have been a womanizer if he hadn't grown up with five sisters. As he was right in the middle in age—two older, three younger—he'd been tutored well in the ways of the female sex. Oh, yes, if anyone at Oxford knew anything about women, it was Mark, and maybe that's why he loved them so much. It's certain that that's why they loved him. John and Sebastian could only stand back and admire the master at work—and happily pick up the dregs he left behind since no man could entertain all women at once. Sebastian would woo them with his French, and John with his clever charm.

And so it was that John Welles found himself in such exalted company on his way down to London for a few day's holiday from classes.

The first stop for the trio, naturally, had been to the tailors, where the week before they had each put in an order for a new waistcoat. Sebastian and Mark had also purchased new coats in the most fashionable styles. Sebastian's had large brass buttons, Mark's had smaller buttons but two rows of them, looking very smart, indeed. Sadly, John couldn't afford the expense, so he made do with what he had, but that was all right. He knew that once his friends had attracted the attention of some lovely ladies, at least one would feel sorry for him and he wouldn't be left out of the fun. It was the way it usually happened when they went out—some girls even liked a quieter type, or so they said.

Decked out in their new finery, the trio headed to Lady Blakemore's ball. She was known to be a stickler for propriety, and while it was true that none of the young men actually possessed an invitation, who was going to turn away three handsome, eligible peers? John also claimed to be there to chaperone his sister, who, he was sure, would be in attendance even though he hadn't actually spoken with her.

The elder two of Mark's sisters would probably be there as well, but he didn't point that out to the footman at the door as he was pretty certain he didn't actually want to meet them for fear that his mother would find out that he wasn't where he was supposed to be—at school.

John felt that since he had just claimed to be chaperoning his sister, he'd better look for her first. It was a pity he knew precisely where to look.

"Search behind all the plants," he instructed his friends, "and along the walls."

Sebastian gave a little laugh. "Like you, is she?"

"Worse!" John said, not finding the fact amusing at all. He, at least, was trying to be more bold and outgoing. Louise, he was certain, wouldn't even make an attempt. It had taken their mother nearly two years of nagging and bullying, and then finally an edict from their father to get Louise to make her debut in society at all.

"I think I see her," Mark said, with his back to John. "Is that her over there by the doors to the garden in the dress with the high neckline?"

John turned to see where his friend was looking. He was so happy—relieved, even, to see her talking with two other young ladies. They were even laughing, although it was odd because Louise wasn't. She was looking distinctly uncomfortable and unhappy.

"Well, that's promising," Sebastian said. "She's talking with those two girls."

Mark nodded. "Diamonds of the first water, I'd say," he said, a smile spreading on his face.

But even as they watched, the girls burst into laughter, turned their back on Louise and walked away. Louise's face flushed bright pink and turned her face to the wall.

"I'll kill them," John said quietly, starting toward the girls who'd clearly just been horridly rude and cut his sister.

A hand grabbed his arm and pulled him back. "No, we don't confront ill-mannered girls," Mark said quietly. "We get even. Come on."

He led the way to Louise's side. Louise was pretty enough but fair when dark-haired beauty was more valued, and curvy when slender and willowy figures were shown to greater advantage by current fashions.

"Just behave normally," Mark advised as they neared her.

John gave him a nod, hoping that his friend knew what he was doing.

"You really shouldn't hide, you know," John said, by way of greeting, trying to act as if he hadn't seen what had just happened.

"Johnny!" Louise exclaimed and then nearly threw her arms around her brother before he stopped her.

"Not here, Lou, not the thing, you know," John said. "May I present my friends, the Marquess of Cenway and the Earl of Thetford. Miss Louise Welles."

Louise curtsied properly. Sebastian bowed, but Mark reached out and took Louise's hand placing a kiss on her gloved fingers.

"What an honor it is to finally make your acquaintance, Miss Welles. John has told us all about you," Mark said, curving his lips up into a smile that John had seen girls swoon over.

His sister was clearly no different. Her mouth dropped open just a touch, and two spots of color brightened her cheeks.

"Oh, dear," she finally said, pulling herself together. She glanced at John. "I do hope John hasn't bored you to tears by talking about me?"

"*Never* boring, my dear Miss Welles," Mark said.

"He's told us about how you've actually increased the productivity of your father's lands by applying some new agricultural methods," Sebastian said with a broad smile.

John couldn't believe his friend had even remembered that. It had to have been at least a month since he'd mentioned his sister's agricultural pursuits.

"Goodness knows, my estate could use some of your forward thinking," Mark added.

"Oh," Louise put a hand to her cheek and actually giggled. "I'm sure that we shouldn't be discussing such practical matters at a ball, gentlemen."

"Perhaps not, but I can't say when I've had the pleasure—"

"Good evening, my lords," a woman's voice said.

John and his friends turned to see the same two girls who had been plaguing Louise earlier had returned.

"Why, good evening, ladies," Mark said smoothly.

The girls both looked to Louise to introduce them, but she actually pressed her lips together.

One of them glared at her and then pasted a polite smile onto her face. "Aren't you going to introduce us to your friends, Miss Welles?"

Louise had no choice. "Miss Enderlin and Miss Wheston," she said and then turned to Mark next to her. "This is the Earl of Thetford." She paused while Mark bowed to the girls. "And the Marquess of Cenway."

"Enchantée," Sebastian said, bowing to the two girls. They giggled in response, as girls always did.

"And the Honorable—"

"Wait, you introduced the earl before the marquess?" Miss Enderlin said, interrupting Louise. "Don't you know anything?"

"You always introduce gentlemen by order of rank," Miss Wheston agreed.

"You gentlemen will have to excuse our, well, I would say friend, but perhaps acquaintance is more like it. Clearly, she hasn't been properly taught how to go on in society," Miss Enderlin said with a harsh tone to her voice. She must have meant for the three men to think poorly of Louise, but all John could do was steam silently and bite his tongue while Mark gave him a warning look.

"And you, who insult a girl to her face and in front of three strangers, have better manners?" Sebastian said, lifting one eyebrow and looking down his nose at the women.

"Ah…" Miss Enderlin said, turning slightly pale.

"Well, we certainly wouldn't do so with anyone who *mattered*," Miss Wheston said quickly.

"Did you just say that we didn't matter?" Mark asked before he burst out laughing.

"Oh, no! Not at all!" Miss Enderlin objected as color rushed back into her cheeks.

"No, it is Miss Welles we were referring to. Naturally, you three gentlemen matter a *great* deal," Miss Wheston agreed.

"And what makes you think Miss Welles does not?" John asked trying to keep the growl of fury from his voice.

"Oh, well, because she does nothing but stand by the wall," Miss Wheston said.

"She never even dances or pay morning calls," Miss Enderlin added.

"She's barely a member of society," Miss Wheston agreed.

"I can't imagine how she even received an invitation to this ball," Miss Enderlin finished.

"I see, and so instead of helping a fellow young lady who is shy and unsure of herself, you thought it better to insult her to her face and to us," Mark clarified.

"You couldn't be thinking that such behavior would make you more interesting to us," Sebastian said, incredulously.

"Well..." Miss Enderlin hesitated.

"You know, I have the strangest idea that that is precisely what these women thought—although, to call them ladies—" John started.

"That would be completely misleading," Mark agreed before John had even finished his sentence.

"Stupid, shallow and mean," Sebastian summed up neatly what John was thinking, although in much more polite language.

"Miss Welles, I do believe a dance is about to begin," Mark said, turning his back on the two girls who were standing there dumbfounded and looking decidedly pale. "Would you do me the honor?" He finished, holding out his hand to Louise.

"Oh, thank you, my lord," Louise said, giving him a hesitant smile and a curtsy before taking his hand.

The other two young ladies had disappeared by the time John and Sebastian turned back from watching them go.

"Well, Mark was right, they *were* considered diamonds," Sebastian commented.

"I think I prefer emeralds," John said, turning back to watch his sister sparkle with his friend's attention.

Look for the next book in the Ladies' Wagering Whist Society
THE GAMES SHE PLAYED

Can the Ladies' Wagering Whist Society help an extroverted sportswoman and a dedicated scientist solve matters of the heart?

Diana Hemshawe is enjoying the perfect life—her first season in Regency society, racing her beloved horse, and the companionship of the ladies of the Wagering Whist Society. When her father has a heart attack, she has to refocus her energies on nursing him back to health. Balancing responsibilities shouldn't be too difficult for someone as resourceful as Diana ... except for the charming and thoughtful doctor who is so very distracting.

Andrew, Lord Colburn, used to be passionate about just one thing—pursuing the cutting edge of medical research. Now his excitement in discovering a new cure for his patient's heart disease is warring with his growing fascination with the man's clever and spirited daughter. But can he learn to balance his loyalty to patients with his desire for her?

It will take all the guile of the Ladies' Wagering Whist Society to ensure that Andrew and Diana have a sporting chance at love.

ABOUT THE AUTHOR

Meredith Bond's books straddle that beautiful line between historical romance and fantasy. An award-winning author, she writes fun traditional Regency romances, medieval Arthurian romances, and Regency romances with a touch of magic. Known for her characters "who slip readily into one's heart," Meredith's heart belongs to her husband and two children.

Meredith loves connecting with readers. Sign up for her monthly newsletter at http://meredithbond. com/blog/newsletter-sign-up/ to receive free short stories and get all her news before anyone else. And don't forget to find her on-line:

Website: http://www.meredithbond.com
Facebook:
https://www.facebook.com/meredithbondauthor
Twitter: https://twitter.com/merrybond
Pinterest:
http://www.pinterest.com/merrybond/
Amazon:
http://www.amazon.com/Meredith-Bond/e/B001KI1SNE
Instagram:
https://www.instagram.com/meredith_bond/
Bookbub:
https://www.bookbub.com/authors/meredith-bond
Newsletter:
http://meredithbond.com/subscribe/

Please don't forget to leave a review wherever you buy books.

Follow all of the women of the Ladies' Wagering Whist Society

1806 Season
A Hand for the Duke
Featuring Christianne Norman, Lady Norman
The Jack of Diamonds
Featuring Miss Lydia Sheffield
The Games She Played
Featuring Miss Diana Hemshawe

1807 Season
A Trick of Mirrors
Featuring Claire Tyne, Lady Blakemore
A Bid for Romance
Featuring Alys Russell, Duchess of Kendell
An Affair of Hearts
Featuring Mrs. Penelope Aldridge

1808 Season
Love in Spades
Featuring Cynthia Montley, Lady Sorrell
A Token of Love
Featuring Ellen Aston, Lady Moreton
The King of Clubs
Featuring Joshua Powell, Lord Wickford

Other Books By Meredith Bond